DISSIPATE

BRITTANY TAYLOR

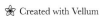 Created with Vellum

OTHER TITLES BY BRITTANY TAYLOR

Without You

Without Me

Mine: A Back to Me Series Book 2

Back to Me: A Back to Me Series Book 3

What Are the Chances

See Through

All available through Kindle Unlimited!

For Ashley
Thank you for bringing out my crazy
Thank you for pushing me to bring this book to the next level
And more importantly, thank you for being my best friend

Dissipate

ONE

In *Mont Saint-Victoire,* Paul Cezanne sought to explore the

   A) fleeting atmospheric effects of changing light

   B) co-existence of multiple viewpoints in a single scene

   C) presentation of space as an extension of the painter's psyche

   D) harmonious effects of an analogous color scheme

I TAP MY PENCIL AGAINST MY SMALL WOODEN DESK, SLOWLY reading out each answer in my head. I don't even have to read all the options to know which one is the correct one. Are they fucking kidding? This question is too easy. They all are.

I'm the smartest person in this class. Shit, I'm probably the smartest person to ever graduate from the Art Degree program at Brown University.

Well, I haven't graduated yet, but I'm not worried. I'm already sporting a perfect 4.0 GPA, and after spending the last two hours breezing through my final, I've already imagined walking across that stage a thousand times.

I glance up at the clock and realize I still have ten minutes to spare—as if it were somehow different from every other test I've taken. Already bored, I leave the bubble unfilled, deciding to wait until the last minute. I don't want to seem too eager to finish my test. Instead, I glance around the room and study my class-mates. They're the ones who should be worried. They're the ones who should be sweating balls, wondering if they're going to have to spend the next four months of their lives repeating this absurdly easy Art History class. Pathetic. Every single one of them.

Correction, there's one exception. There's only one who doesn't belong in this grotesque group of stupidity—my girlfriend, Lena.

I rest my chin in my hand and continue looking around the room.

Everyone's heads are bent down, intently focused on the booklet in front of them, including Lena. Her desk is two rows down from mine. From the first day of class at the beginning of the semester, she insisted sitting as far away from me as possible. She said I would distract her, and she would distract me. And she was fucking right. Even with her being two rows in front of me, she still distracts me. No amount of space would change that fact. She might as well be sitting in my lap, both of her legs wrapped around my waist, her riding my cock like she does every other fucking day.

She's fucking gorgeous. Her tan skin glows against the dull lights of the classroom, her long blonde hair swept to the side, resting over her shoulder. Concentrating on the test in front of her, she absentmindedly runs her fingertips through the ends and tucks her bottom lip under her teeth, gently biting down. She presses the tip of her number two pencil to the sheet, filling in one of the small bubbles. She's still playing with the ends of her golden blonde hair when she glances over her shoulder, looking at me.

When her eyes finally land on me, she catches me staring

straight at her. I grin at the same time a smile spreads across her face, her eyes a pale brown, bordering a grey-violet shade.

"Already finished?" she mouths.

I tap my pencil against the desk again and smirk. She must already know the answer to her own question because she starts to slowly shake her head. My eyes immediately focus on her mouth —that gorgeous fucking mouth. Remembering the way her full lips have pressed against my skin causes my stomach to twist with a pleasuring ache. I grow hard for her, the pressure building in my jeans. Slouched in my seat, I adjust my pants, hoping to at least relieve some of the pressure until the end of class. Until I can get Lena alone.

"Yes," I mouth back.

Shaking her head again, she scoffs, then turns back around. She props her elbow on her desk and rests her head in her hand, shielding me from being able to see her face. She's smart, she's always been smart. So, when I look back down at my test and fill in the bubble for the last question, I know she's going to pass with flying fucking colors—just like me.

When I'm finished, I take one more look at my classmates. Fucking idiots. Every single one of them.

Closing my booklet, I wait out the last minute, watching the clock above the professor's desk, counting along as the minute hand ticks. The second it lands on the twelve, my professor stands up, walking around his desk.

"Time's up. Pencil's down, close your tests," he announces.

I sigh, relieved to have finally finished this class. For the past four months, I've spent countless hours studying, reading, and socializing with more than half of the people in this room. I didn't want to spend time with them, but Lena convinced me we had to if we wanted to get the most out of the class. If I wanted to gain the most experience to prepare for my career. I don't believe in failure, and I would be damned if one of these fucking assholes was the reason I didn't pass this class with a perfect score. So, I did what I had to do. I mustered as much decency I could, which if

I'm honest, wasn't very much. And it was hard as hell, too. My tolerance for ill-behavior was thin, very thin.

I didn't like to drink much, but these assholes seemed to feel the need to drink every time we got together. I couldn't stand it. And by the end of the night, after hours of studying, I seemed to be the only sober one out of the group. Most of the nights, Lena had let herself loose—in more ways than one.

I guess, in hindsight, maybe our study sessions weren't a complete form of punishment. I was always rewarded with Lena in my bed. She never insisted on going back to her place as she usually did if she were sober, and I never argued.

After turning in my test, I meet Lena by the front door of the classroom. She's waiting for me as always. She's wearing black jeans, torn at the knees, and a grey, jersey knit t-shirt. The fabric of her pale grey shirt stretches across her breasts, accentuating their perfect round curves.

I wrap my arm around her waist, pulling her beside me as we walk down the hallway. Tipping my head to the side, I whisper in her ear, "You look abso-fucking-lutely gorgeous today." Giggling, she looks down at her feet. We step outside, the afternoon sun shining brightly.

"One thing," I add. "I wish it was a V-neck instead." Reaching across her, I hook my index finger around the collar of her scoop neck tee and pull down.

Stopping on the sidewalk, she yanks her body away from me, her eyes spread wide, and her jaw drops. She adjusts her shirt, her hands jerking with every movement.

"Julian Price, what the fuck is wrong with you?"

Placing her hand over her chest, she looks around, scanning the parking lot and street for anyone who might have seen.

I hold my hand out to her. "You're being dramatic. I didn't pull it down that far."

Scoffing, she adjusts the strap of the messenger bag draped across her shoulder. "You can be such an asshole sometimes,

Julian." Her mumble fades as she quickly passes me, leaving me standing on the sidewalk.

"Wait." Jogging up behind her, I wrap my arms around her waist, and feel her body sag against me. She blows out a hot breath, stopping. Resting my chin on her shoulder, I can feel her hesitance. I don't say another word, pulling her farther into me, her back pressing against my chest. I kiss her shoulder, feeling the warmth of her shoot straight through me.

She steps forward, forcing my arms to slide away from her body. She turns around, her mouth set in a frown, her eyebrows slanted, her eyes lit with fire. She's still angry with me, but I don't care. In the two years I've been with Lena, I quickly learned she never stays angry for long. Our relationship is fucking perfect, everything about us is perfect. Knowing she'll only ever be mine— no other asshole can take away what I have.

So, I'm not worried about shit when Lena steps away from me and crosses her arms over her chest in a huff. Her pink lips are still set into a frown as her arms squeeze tightly around her middle, pushing up her breasts. I bite my tongue, still wishing it was a V-neck and not a fucking scoop neck.

Smirking, I step forward, reaching my hand out, touching her arm with my fingertips, feeling her perfectly smooth milky skin.

"Lena..."

"I'm serious, Julian," she says, cutting me off. She steps away from me, breaking our touch.

"Lena, you know I didn't mean it." I'm lying. I meant it. Other than the fit of the shirt against her lean body, I hate the shirt. I don't understand why she even bothers wearing it. Doesn't she want to show her body off? She should because I want her to.

I lie because I want her to let this go. I need her to let this go. Lena's a beautiful, twenty-two-year-old woman—even when she's angry. But I don't like the way her anger makes me feel. As if I've done something wrong.

I swallow my words, digesting them before I allow myself to

5

speak. There are only a handful of times I've uttered these words. And ninety percent of them were said to Lena.

She sighs, her shoulders sagging. Her eyes briefly close as she waits for the words she wishes were coming. I can see it hidden behind her still rigid small frame. She wants me to apologize. Fucking women.

Inhaling a hot breath, I grant her wish. "I'm sorry." I lift my hand, ready to rest my palm against her cheek.

My arm is halfway raised when she asks.

"Sorry for what, exactly?"

"Lena, this is ridiculous," I sigh. "You know what I'm sorry for." I reach for her again when my hand finally meets her warm cheek. My fingertips rest by her ear, touching her soft blonde hair. I look into her eyes, willing her to not make me repeat it.

Even with her standing in front of me, still angry, I force myself to remain calm. She knows why it's difficult for me to apologize for anything. I live my life according to what I believe in, what I was raised to believe in. And apologizing was one of those things that was never expected in my household—unless it was to my father. He was the only one who ever demanded an apology and never gave one. Always take, never give, that was one of his rules.

I brush the thoughts of my arrogant, asshole, piece-of-shit father out of my mind and stare at the love of my life—the only thing that makes sense in this world.

"I shouldn't have pulled your shirt down," I quickly say. I narrow my eyes and stare at her with a straight face. "There, are you happy now?"

Draping her arms around my neck, she weaves her fingers through my blonde hair. "Thank you." Leaning forward and standing on her toes, she brings her mouth to mine. Barely brushing my lips, she whispers, "Mr. Price."

My cock hardens at her use of calling me Mr. Price. I feel like a fucking king, and she's just handed me my crown.

"I fucking love you, Ms. Quinn."

Her lips part slightly, and her eyes widen. It's not the first time we've said I love you, so I take her reaction as more of a surprise for saying it so bluntly in public. The occasional student passes us, some deep in conversation, most focused on their phones resting in their hand. I ignore every one of them as I listen to her breaths. Her chest moves against mine, the flesh of her breasts pressing against me once again.

Closing the space between our mouths, I claim hers with mine. A gasp escapes her, surprised at my sudden movement. She parts her lips, fully welcoming me as her tongue slides against mine. She tastes sweet as if she's just eaten vanilla ice cream. I grip her waist, digging my fingers into the soft, supple flesh of her curves. She's the perfect size. Her waist is small, small enough for me to wrap my arm completely around her. I slide my hands down her slim waist and rest them just above her full, round ass. Moaning against me, I press my hips into her. My hardened cock presses into her lower belly, feeling the waist of her tight black jeans push against me.

"Fuck, Lena," I groan, wanting more of her and now.

She pulls away from me, her hands still gripping my arms. My muscles tense under her touch. Her breaths are short and heavy. Her mouth curls into a smirk.

"What is it, Mr. Price?"

She's playing with me, and I fucking love it. Her pale brown eyes fill with desire and delight, waiting for me to respond. I can see it. She wants me just as bad as I want her. Too bad we aren't somewhere more private.

Maybe I could take her behind one of the trees or buildings, and no one would notice.

Tempted as I may be, I remember my ability to bring out noises in Lena that would be considered inappropriate when made in public.

I drop my gaze, narrowing my eyes.

"I'm thinking we celebrate tonight." I'm hoping my change of subject will take my mind off my still present erection. "I say we go to Bar Americano for some dinner, then..." Stepping forward, I place my hands back onto her hips and pull her forward. I pull her hard enough to where her body slams against mine, and her stomach presses into my crotch. *Fuck, I shouldn't have done that.* "...then after dinner, we head back to my place."

Lena's eyes widened the second I pressed her body into mine, but now as I finish my offer to spoil the fuck out of her tonight to celebrate both of us finally finishing our classes, her eyes sadden, and her body relaxes. I've been with Lena long enough to know what she's about to say. I bite back the urge to stop her from speaking. The familiar burn beneath my skin tingles, awakening a mixture of anger and disappointment.

"Sorry, baby." She pouts her bottom lip, her lip gloss glistening against the afternoon sun. "I already told Abby I would meet her for dinner."

Annoyed, I take a step back. I knew it. I fucking knew it.

"Really, Lena? Abby?" I scoff and rake my fingers through my hair, pushing it back and to the side. "You would rather celebrate with Abby than me, your own fucking boyfriend?"

Backing up even farther, she drops her shoulder. I can tell she's already prepared for this conversation. She knows what I'm going to say.

She sighs and opens her mouth to answer my questions, but I stop her before she gets the chance to say a word.

"You know what, Lena? It seems like you don't have time to see me at all anymore."

"What are you talking about, Julian?" Crossing her arms over her chest, she narrows her eyes right back at me. ""What are you talking about, Julian? We see each other all the time. We live in the same fucking town, literally blocks away from each other. We have nearly half the same classes. So, please, tell me how you never see me?"

Closing the space between us, I stand in front of her. A sharp breath escapes her as the tip of my nose touches hers. I bite the inside of my cheek, forcing myself to stay calm.

"Come on, Lena." My voice is low and slow, making sure she hears every word. "You'll have a better time celebrating with me, and you know it."

I keep the part out about where I don't agree with her choice of friends. Lena and I met Abby a few years back in one of our classes. I didn't care for her too much, but there was something about her that caught Lena's attention. Abby seemed stuck up as if she was better than I was, I could tell. But unlike Abby, I know the truth. I know I'm better than her, and she doesn't deserve Lena's attention or friendship.

She sighs, pressing her lips together and frowns. She's giving me nothing but silence as I watch her, knowing she's deciding what to do. Her vacant eyes search me. She's looking at me but she isn't.

"Come on." I smile, swaying her hips side to side, urging her to agree.

Finally, her eyes break away from my chest as she looks up at me. With a heavy sigh, she offers me a weak smile.

"Fine, I'll call Abby and tell her we can hang out tomorrow."

"Great." I plant a kiss on her forehead and lean back. "Meet me at the restaurant at seven."

"Okay." She offers me a small nod in agreement.

"Seriously," I begin walking backward, leaving her standing on the sidewalk. "Don't be late. You know I hate that."

"I know."

Before I turn around and head in the direction of my car, I grip the strap of my brown leather messenger bag resting across my shoulder. With a smirk, I look her up and down, taking in her whole body.

"Oh, and might I make one little suggestion?" My eyes dance across her fully clothed body. Everything from her long black skinny jeans, to that goddamn grey, scoop neck t-shirt. "Wear something a bit more, well... less."

I don't bother waiting for her response, already knowing she'll take my suggestion. She always does.

9

TWO

I smooth my hand across the white linen tablecloth, feeling it slide along the skin of my hand. I straighten my fork and spoon just as the waiter approaches my table.

"Good evening, sir. Are you meeting someone?"

"Yes," I say, clearing my throat. "My girlfriend should be here any minute."

"Great," he smiles. "Would you like to start with something to drink while you wait?"

"Yes. Two glasses and a bottle of your most expensive Cabernet."

"Right away, sir." The waiter nods with his hands clasped behind his back, his long black apron tied around his waist. Without another word, he turns around and disappears behind the swinging door to the kitchen.

Bar Americano is my favorite restaurant in Providence. As I look around at all the white linen-topped tables, each adorned with one tall white candle and a rose, I think of my hometown. Not because this restaurant reminds me of home—quite the opposite. I wouldn't consider Providence one of the classiest cities in America. It isn't quite as large and opulent as say, New York

City or even Boston. However, it is steps above Baton Rouge, Louisiana.

I pick my phone up from the table and look at the time. 7:02. Lena's late.

Turning over my phone, I sit back in my seat and slam it down onto the table. My phone makes a dull thud as it hits the cushioned, fabric-lined, wooden table.

A flash of purple fills the corner of my eye near the direction of the front door. I spot Lena as she hands the hostess her coat and walks over to me, the shiny fabric of her purple cocktail dress hugging her every curve. Sitting here, watching Lena, I would say I've come a long way from the trailer parks of Baton Rouge.

The closer Lena gets to our table, I lean back in my chair and tap my fingers against the table top. With my other hand, I smooth my hand down my black tie and take a deep breath.

I'm still looking down at my chest as Lena pulls out her chair and sets her silver clutch on top of the table, beside her plate.

"Hey, baby," she says, her voice light, happy even.

Annoyed, I look up and stare into her eyes. "You're late."

Sitting back in her chair, she looks off to the side, avoiding my stare.

"Come on, Julian. Don't start. We're supposed to be celebrating."

"Well, it would be much easier to celebrate if you were here on time." I lean forward, resting my arms on the edge of the table. "And it would be less embarrassing if I didn't have to tell our waiter my girlfriend wasn't here yet."

Rolling her eyes, she scoffs. I can tell she's annoyed with me, but I'm even more annoyed with her. She embarrassed me, and she needs to understand how it feels.

She clicks her tongue, still avoiding my gaze. "You are being absolutely ridiculous."

"I told you seven, Lena." I ball my hand into a fist, watching the skin of my knuckles turn from a pale pink to white. I clench my jaw, feeling the pressure of my teeth grinding against one another. "Is it so fucking hard to follow a simple schedule?"

Finally turning toward me, she steels her eyes to mine. Her lips are painted a shiny pink, but when she slides her tongue across her bottom lip, it completely disappears, leaving her lips bare and natural. I fight back the urge to lean across the table and bite her lip, remembering what we're discussing in the first place.

"I can't believe I ditched Abby for this. You do realize I canceled plans with her tonight, right? To be with you?" Leaning forward, she whispers, "You're being an asshole, Julian."

I clench my jaw even tighter, her words traveling straight through me. My skin tingles and my heart races. I lean forward, matching her movements. She leans back the moment I get closer to her, her eyes spread wide.

I narrow my eyes and tilt my head to the side, allowing the silence to fall between us. The faint sound of clinking glasses and silverware grating against porcelain dishes fades into the background.

"What did you just say?" I seethe.

Lena's neck dips as she swallows, her eyes lining with tears. She's on the verge of crying, and I can tell she's fighting back because she knows how much I hate when she cries. The fabric of her dress moves along with her steady, heavy breaths. Her tan skin glistens under the golden lights, and I find myself wishing she didn't put me in this position. I wish our conversation was headed in a different direction.

Another minute of silence passes when she finally whispers, "Nothing. I didn't mean it."

Smiling, I lean back and reposition my tie just as the waiter finally returns to our table,

placing two empty glasses in front of us. Lena and I watch him in silence as he opens our bottle before pouring a small amount in my glass.

I swirl the smooth red liquid, watching as it glides across the clear glass. After taking a sip and feeling the liquid slide across my tongue, burning its way down my throat, I nod, assuring the waiter it's the right wine.

He fills Lena's glass halfway before returning to mine, filling it to match hers. He sets the bottle down and turns toward Lena. "Are you all set to order, ma'am?"

Lena tips her chin up, looking up to the waiter standing between us. She purses her lips and twists her mouth to the side in thought. "Um, I think—"

"No," I interrupt. "*We're* not ready to order yet." I pin my eyes on Lena.

"Of course." The waiter says, clearing his throat, obviously realizing he fucked up. "I'll give you two a few more minutes."

Jesus. How anyone could stand to work as anyone's server is beyond me.

Nodding again, the waiter ducks his head and shuffles back to the kitchen in silence.

"I'm sorry. I didn't realize you weren't ready to order yet." Lena's voice is small, and I'm thankful I don't have to bring up her lack of regard for me.

I twist my fork still resting on my white linen napkin, willing this dinner to go the way I want it to. All I wanted to do was celebrate us and our successes of finally finishing our classes. But so far, all I've gotten is a tardy Lena and a waiter who can't seem to keep his eyes off of my girlfriend.

Inhaling a deep breath, I close my eyes before opening them back on Lena.

"It's fine," I say, brushing away my frustrations. *I will make this a good night.*

Wrapping my fingers around the stem of my glass, I raise it in the air and hold it out to Lena. She's still sitting back in her chair, one leg crossed over the other, her arms draped over her legs.

I press my lips together, releasing a hot breath. Why must she be so difficult? I nod my head toward her glass, urging her to pick it up.

She hesitates, her chest clearly rising and falling with every agonizing second that passes. Finally, she sits up and grabs the stem of her glass, resting her elbow on the table.

I smile, thinking of today. I think of all the work I've put in the past few years. And I think of that trailer back in Baton Rouge. Those thoughts lead me to my father. I smile at Lena, knowing I showed that motherfucker. The moment I was accepted into Brown University when I was eighteen years old and left that godforsaken trailer park, I knew I had already done better than my father ever could have imagined. And I had proven him to be wrong.

If I could, I would shove my successes in my father's face. But I know I don't have to, knowing he's rotting in the ground in some back-country cemetery in Baton Rouge.

Still, I smile at Lena, proud of how far we've come.

She offers me a simple, small smile in return.

Clearing my throat, I raise my voice just above the clanking of silverware and music playing overhead.

"To us," I start. "To finishing our final *final*." I pause, listening to a reluctant giggle erupt from Lena's throat. I've coaxed a small laugh out of her and a small knot in the pit of my stomach twists. It's odd because I feel like I should be relieved she's laughing at my joke. I should be happy that she's happy. But something hidden in those light brown eyes of hers tells me otherwise.

I can't put my finger on it, but years of being with the same woman and learning every tick and mannerism leaves me with somewhat of a bit of knowledge to these things.

Such as her subtle movements, the ones where she nervously swallows even when she hasn't taken a drink of her wine. The moments where her smooth, black dusted eyelids blink more than they usually do. And the ones where her breaths grow increasingly more frequent and shallow.

She doesn't think I notice these things. But I do. I love Lena, always have. I've loved her since she walked into my painting class junior year. It didn't take much to convince her to go out on a date with me. She was the hottest fucking woman I'd ever seen, and unlike most people who think they can be artists, Lena actually was one. She was good. Real fucking good.

She was meant for me, and I knew it.

"So," I say, still holding my glass between us. "To you, Lena. For being the smartest, sexiest, and most talented woman I know." I make sure to send her a wink before I add, "And to me."

Her mouth spreads into a flat thin smile as I bring my glass to my mouth, drinking a large sip of my dark red wine.

Lena follows suit, drinking nearly half her glass before she places it back in front of her. She licks her lips and looks at me again.

I push my plate aside and lean forward, resting my arms on the table.

"Well?"

"What?" she asks.

"I can tell you're keeping something from me. Are you going to tell me what it is, or do I have to guess what it is?"

She sits forward, sliding her plate forward with her bright red painted fingertips. She crosses her arms over the table and leans toward me, her breasts pressed together between her arms. Her purple dress dips in the front, the bottom of her neckline plunging all the way down below her breast bone. God, I'm so glad she listened to me earlier.

She clears her throat and glances down at the table before looking back up at me. "I spoke with a friend of mine back home."

"Boston?"

"Yes." Lena takes a deep breath. The curiosity of where this conversation might lead me excites me almost as much as the dress she's wearing. *Almost.*

"My friend, Scarlett, I knew her in high school. We parted ways when she decided to go to Harvard, and I decided to go here. Anyway, she says there's an exhibit in a couple weeks at The Institute of Contemporary Art. Opening night is on Friday, the seventeenth." She shrugs. "I thought you'd like to go with me."

I tap my finger on the table and nod, thinking of her invite. I ignore the fact until this moment, Lena has never mentioned Scarlett before. Maybe they aren't as close friends as she is with Abby. I wonder if she's smarter than Abby—God, I hope so—or else that would mean my girlfriend has very bad judgment in her choice of friends.

Lena grew up in the classy suburbs of Boston. Unlike my father, hers was one of Boston's most prestigious and aggressive litigation lawyers. Her mother stayed at home, raising her and her sister, Hailey.

And unlike me, Lena didn't run from her hometown. She had nothing to run away from, nothing to hide. Her ties back home still ran somewhat deep. Irritation sears itself beneath the surface of my skin. I hate thinking about Lena's background.

But then I think about The Institute of Contemporary Art. I've never been, but as I've heard and read, it's one of the best museums in the entire country. And it's right up my alley being as it's a contemporary art museum. The potential to make some important career connections would definitely be available.

"After graduation?" I ask, knowing it might help me scope out any job opportunities. It gives me time to prepare for what's out there.

"Yes," she slowly replies.

Smirking, I smile at Lena, the flickering flame of our candle dancing between us.

"Count me in."

"Great." Sending me another closed mouth grin, she picks up her wine glass and brings it to her lips. Again, I'm able to sense her hesitation. Something tells me that wasn't what she was keeping from me.

I open my mouth to ask her what else, but I'm unable to speak when the waiter comes back to our table.

We haven't even looked at our menus, but I bite back my urge to snap at him. I figure if we don't order now, he'll continue to come back and interrupt Lena and my celebration.

"Are you both ready to order?"

Lena sits back and looks at me. She keeps her mouth shut, knowing I already know what she likes, and I enjoy ordering for her.

"Yes, we'll both have the filet, medium rare, each with a side of your dragon carrot risotto."

The waiter trades glances between me and Lena before he clears his throat. His sad, wide eyes stare at me before they return to normal. "Yes, sir."

He tilts his head and then begins to turn around.

"Excuse me." I hold my finger up as the waiter slowly turns back around.

"Yes, sir?"

"What's your name? I don't believe you said when I sat down."

His eyes dart between me and Lena once again, and I wish for fuck's sake he would stop doing that. From the corner of my eye, I even notice Lena shifting in her seat, her back straightening and her shoulders turning rigid.

"Logan. My name is Logan."

"Well, Logan." Adjusting in my seat, I sit up and rest my arm on the table, looking up at our waiter. I gesture toward Lena. "You see, me and my girlfriend are celebrating tonight. I understand you're probably just doing your job, but we would greatly appreciate it if you made yourself scarce. We come here quite often so no need for all the extra bullshit. I only ask two things of you, Logan."

Logan nervously swallows, lacing his hands behind him once again. I can tell I'm intimidating him. Good, that means he's getting my point. I hold up my finger.

"The first thing I ask is if you see either of our glasses low, don't ask if we would like a refill, just assume we need one and do it. Got it?"

"Yes. Of course." The corner of his mouth twitches and his eyes narrow, studying me. I wait, making sure he's following what

I'm saying. I also don't miss how his narrowed eyes give a side glance at Lena.

Again? What the fuck?

I raise a second finger. "And two. I would appreciate it if you would stop fucking looking at my girlfriend as if I wasn't sitting right across from her."

"I wasn't." he quickly defends.

I frown and then scoff, tilting my head to the side. "No, you were. But I'll let those go."

"I'll, um." Logan stares at me, swallowing before he continues, "I'll go put your orders in now."

Without another word, Logan hurries off. When I turn my attention back to Lena, she's not looking at me. Instead, she's staring at Logan's back, watching as he disappears to wherever the fuck he goes when he isn't serving his tables. My care for him diminishes when I see a single tear slide down Lena's cheek.

Taking a deep breath, she lifts her hand and wipes it away.

"What?" I ask her. I don't know why she's crying. It's not like I said anything horrible.

She takes another deep breath before turning toward me. Her eyes are filled with pools of tears threatening to spill, but she holds them back, and I can sense in the way her body is rigidly seated, it's taking everything in her to keep them at bay.

"What is it?" I ask again, annoyed.

"Nothing," she whispers. Then as she picks up her wine glass again and tilts it back all the way, allowing the rest of the dark red liquid to wash down her throat, I see it.

I see the secrets she's keeping from me. I may not know what they are, but I know they're there.

Logan only came back to our table two more times. The first time was to bring us our food. Luckily, our steak was cooked to perfection, and the risotto was like pure velvet in my mouth, so I didn't need to pull Logan aside. The second time he came back was when he dropped off the check. He didn't steal another glance at Lena. Good thing too because I don't know what would have happened if he had.

Lena and I spent the rest of dinner in polite and light conversation. Mostly we discussed what kinds of art we would see at the museum in Boston next week and how we felt about our graduation coming up. I was excited about what the future held for us. By the time dessert came around, I was thrilled when Lena started acting more like herself. She was laughing at my jokes again, and the light had returned to her beautiful eyes.

Although the dinner had gone fantastic as I knew it would, there was still that same feeling gnawing at the back of my mind. The feeling Lena was keeping secrets from me.

After the check is paid, I walk Lena to her car, parked on the opposite side of the lot from mine.

Pinning her against her car with my hips, I grip the back of her head and pull her in for a kiss. She places her hands on my hips, sliding them beneath my suit jacket, her hands grazing my abs, causing my erection to grow.

She digs her nails into my sides, full well knowing what it does to me.

I let out a growl when I slide my tongue between her lips. She opens her mouth, allowing me to possess hers. She tastes like wine and the chocolate cake we had for dessert.

I press my hips into her again as I tilt her head up, pressing my lips to her neck. She breathes heavily, gripping my white collared shirt.

With my lips pressed against the warm, damp skin of her neck, I whisper, "Come to my place tonight. Stay with me."

I'm begging, and I hate to beg. But Lena is the one exception —the only exception.

"I can't," she giggles.

I thread my fingers through her silky hair, her scent filling my nose.

Dragging my nose across her cheek, I breathe her in once

again. Her skin is soft like velvet against mine. I want to bury myself in her and never come up for air.

Pressing my fingers into the base of her neck, I kiss her once on the lips, then pull away, staring into her eyes.

"And why not?"

She sighs, briefly closing her eyes. "It's been a long day, Julian. I'm tired. Between classes and all my finals, I'm wiped out."

Her hands slide up and down my lower back and my skin tingles.

Slightly pulling away from her, I glance down. "And what am I supposed to do about this?"

Following my gaze, she laughs before she moves her hand to the waist of my pants, dipping her finger between my pants and my shirt. Moving her hand, she slides her finger to my stomach, stopping below my belly button. She lifts her thigh, pressing between my legs. I growl, my dick growing harder with her teasing.

"You can come over tomorrow morning, and we'll take care of it." Hooking her finger on the waist of my pants, she jerks me forward. Her lips ghost mine, the lingering taste of cabernet still soaked into her mouth.

Leaning forward and closing the small space between us, I graze my tongue along her lips, tasting what's left of the wine on her mouth. "Sounds good to me." I kiss her one last time before reluctantly pulling away.

"I love you, Lena Quinn," I say, backing away toward the other side of the parking lot.

Giving me a half smile, she says, "You too."

When I make it to my car and pull out of the restaurant parking lot, I find myself not far behind Lena.

The bright red glow of her brake lights reflects off the water droplets still sprinkled across my windshield. The rain has stopped, but the air is thick with moisture. A fine mist lingers, and every few minutes, I turn on my wipers, giving me a fresh view of Lena's car in front of me.

The street lights of downtown Providence cascade across my damp car like a constant moving film reel. One second the light is there, the next it's gone.

My fingers wrap around my steering wheel, gripping it tighter. My knuckles turn white. I'm lucky it's dark out so Lena wouldn't be able to see me as easily if it were daytime. But my black BMW is still somewhat recognizable, especially to someone like Lena.

As expected, she turns into the parking lot of her apartment, parking in her designated spot reserved for apartment 514.

I park my car along the opposite row from Lena's spot but several cars down. Far down enough to where I know she can't see me. I shift in my seat and lean forward, peering through the lingering dots of rain still gathered on my windshield.

More drops land on my windshield, obscuring my view. "For fuck's sake," I say into the dark, flicking on my windshield wipers.

My stomach turns, filled with the anticipation of what's happening. I've always trusted Lena in the two years I've been with her. I'm not ignorant of her beauty or her intelligence. I know how fucking desirable she is, but I also know how she would never betray me. She knows it wouldn't end well if I were to ever find out. She loves me and knows how lucky she is to have a boyfriend like me. I treat her better than any other douchebag, fucker, or asshole out there ever could.

Despite knowing all these things, something in my subconscious is telling me something isn't right. Lena was off tonight. It was those subtle movements of hers, the ones she thinks I didn't notice.

I'm expecting Lena to step out of her car and head up to her apartment. Instead, I find myself leaning farther over my steering wheel, making sure I don't press my body too far into the horn when her face lights up with a bright white light. I can easily tell it's her phone.

Pulling out my phone, I take note of the time. It's late, she shouldn't be out here all by herself. She should get inside to the safety of her apartment. But no, she just sits there. Her face is glowing with colors of white and blue. Then surprisingly, I watch as she lifts her phone, pressing it to her ear.

My phone is still gripped in my hand. I wait for it to ring, knowing she must be calling me because she changed her mind. She does want me to come over. Excitement at the prospect of feeling her limbs and warm flesh wrapped around me tonight heats my very core. Good, I can remind her that she's mine and *only* mine.

I press the button on the side of my phone, wondering why it hasn't started ringing yet. I have at least four bars of good service, and she's literally only feet from me.

But when her lips start moving and her head tips back in laughter, I know she wasn't trying to call me. She's talking to someone else.

THREE

I remember being seven years old, sitting at the edge of my bed in my trailer in Baton Rouge. I didn't have my own room. I stayed in the same room as my parents. Our trailer was small. So small, it only consisted of a living room, a bathroom, a small kitchen, and our bedroom. Our bedroom. My parent's and mine. It was the kind of trailer that was painted a baby blue on the outside and on the inside, had wood paneling covering every square inch of the walls, and dusty matted carpet colored a dingy forest green.

My bed sat on the opposite wall from theirs, a curtain nailed to the ceiling the only dividing piece between me and them.

I didn't understand it at the time, but I remember every Friday and Saturday night, my mother would either send me to spend the night at my friend Nathan's house, just a few trailers over, or when I couldn't stay there, she would put headphones over my ears every night before bed.

One night, I remember sitting on the edge of my bed, dressed in my favorite blue and red pajama set. I remember loving it because of the bright colors. I guess my love for color and art started at a young age. But on this particular night, I remember her placing the overly large headphones over my ears with her cold, shivering hands.

After putting them on, she placed her finger in front of her lips. "Shh, be sure to stay quiet this time, Julian. You know your father doesn't like it when you make noise."

"Okay, Momma."

Grabbing the black cassette player from my nightstand, she plugged in the end of the cord to my headphones and moved my finger over the play button.

"Remember to turn around and face the wall," she whispered, grabbing onto my shoulders. She turned me around and laid me on my side. Leaning forward, she whispered in my ear, the scent of whiskey still lingering on her breath. "Press play the moment you hear the door open." Quickly placing a kiss on my temple, she stood up, closed the curtain, and walked over to her side of the room without another word.

I squeezed my eyes shut, imagining all the places I wanted to go, the Louvre in Paris my biggest dream. I knew one day, I would get there. I would get to see the Mona Lisa. Even at seven years old, I thought she was beautiful.

With my eyes clenched tight, I heard the bedroom door swing open. I didn't immediately press play like my mother said. Mostly because instead of my father coming in quietly, he stormed into the room as if he were angry. I wanted to hear what was about to happen.

"You bitch!" he yelled.

"Christian, just listen," My mother's worried voice quivered. I could hear my father walking farther into the room, felt his presence filling the space behind me. "It's not what you think," my mother added.

"Shut up, you whore!" Then I heard the sound of his hand slapping her skin. At the same time, her body fell to the mattress, and she released a small whimper; my father grunted.

I squeezed my eyes tighter, my finger still hovering over the play button to my cassette player.

"I talked to Ron at the bar," my father seethed. "He told me you fucked him because you couldn't pay your tab. Don't lie to me, Lacey."

"I'm sorry, Christian."

"Fuck your apologies."

I forced myself to keep my eyes shut, unwilling to see what I was hearing. It wasn't new. Most of the time, my father came stumbling into the room, demanding what he wanted. And one hundred percent of the time, he was drunk. That night, he was all the above and then some. He was drunk, demanding, and angrier at my mother than ever before.

That night as I clenched my eyes tighter and clutched the cassette player to my chest, I let one tear slip down my cheek. Quickly wiping it away, just in case my father would see, I curled my legs in tighter and drew closer to the wood-paneled wall. The second the yelling stopped, and I could no longer hear my parents' voices, I hit play on the cassette player.

I stay in my car watching Lena talk on her phone. She's smiling and laughing—smiling and laughing like she does with me. That's the only reason I know it isn't Abby on the other end. This is a different kind of smile, a different kind of laughter. I force myself to stay in my black leather seat, gripping the steering wheel even tighter.

"Fuck!" I slam my palm against the wheel. Releasing a heavy, hot breath, I press my lips into a flat line and rake my fingers through my hair. I push it up and to the side, feeling the cool, moisture-filled air dance across my forehead.

Twenty-one minutes. Twenty-one minutes is how long Lena talks to whichever asshole is on the other end. Finally, just as the time turns to twenty-two minutes, she ends her phone call and turns off her car. Her lights shut off, turning the parking lot to black, the only glow coming from the white moon hanging above us.

I rest my elbow on my car door and sink down slightly in my

seat, pinching the tip of my thumb between my teeth and bite down. My skin stings, but I need the feeling to distract me from what I've seen from Lena tonight. I need to remain calm, despite the growing black cloud raging inside me.

She grabs her small, sparkling clutch and steps out of her car. She doesn't immediately begin walking in, and I hold my breath, still keeping my thumb pinched between my teeth. *What is she doing?*

She stands beside her car and looks up and down the parking lot as if she's looking for someone. Wrapping her arms around herself, she rubs her hands along her arms, almost as if she's cold.

It's okay, Lena. You're safe. There's no one out here but me.

Finally, she presses the lock button on her key fob, causing her lights to blink and a beeping sound to fill the dark night.

Turning around, she makes the short distance to her apartment, and I watch until she walks up to the third floor and disappears into the breezeway.

It takes three minutes to make the drive from Lena's apartment to mine—a small fraction of the time she was on the phone with the mystery person. My mind combs through every possible person Lena knows. She only knows a few people, her circle of friends isn't very large.

So, when I run through the three people I'm certain she talks to on a regular basis and come up with nothing, I slam my hand against the steering wheel again.

Tonight was supposed to be a night of celebration and excitement. Instead, I'm going home alone and with more anger than I know what to do with.

When I make it to the top floor of my building, I exit the elevator and walk to my door with a deep fire in my chest, my head pounding.

I step inside the front door and am met with silence. My apartment is dark, the clean white lines of my kitchen cabinets and bright tile floor glistening in the dark. I toss my keys on the side table and loosen my tie. I think about Lena, and I think about

26

her sitting in front of me in that purple cocktail dress. And I think about her full round breasts, peeking out of the top.

My cock hardens at the thought of her, remembering how the soft flesh of her breasts feels against my tongue, how they taste. Fuck, I need to do something.

Heat evaporates from my body as I remove the rest of my suit, carefully laying it across the foot of my bed. I immediately head toward my bathroom and turn the shower on as hot as it will go. I need to relieve myself of the pressure and consuming thoughts of Lena. I wish she had just fucking let me stay the night. Instead, I let the scorching hot water fill the open space of my walk-in shower. After a few minutes, I wrap my hand around my cock and lean forward, pressing my hand against the tile wall for support. Fuck, that feels good.

My hand slides against my skin as I stroke myself, thinking about the only woman who has ever deserved me.

I think about Lena and her smooth pale skin and her golden blonde hair. My slow movements grow faster, and deeper. Then as I feel myself about to come, I think about Lena and that fucking smile. That fucking smile.

I wake up the next morning, ready to head over to Lena's. I'm still pissed about last night. I'm not even sure what to make of it. It's strange, but I know something isn't right.

But right now, as I'm walking out to my car at eight in the morning, I don't give two shits.

I thought I could take care of my need for Lena last night in the shower, but I still went to bed furious and confused. I can't think about anything but feeling Lena's naked body beneath mine and being inside her. That's what I need—not a hand full of soap and an empty shower.

I made sure to wear a t-shirt and sweatpants when I got dressed this morning. Sweatpants are easier to take off.

I don't bother calling Lena when I wake up, or even on the drive over. I want to surprise her.

When I pull into the parking lot to Lena's apartment, I see her car still parked in the same spot it was last night. My adrenaline picks up, ready to see my girl. After pulling into the first spot I see, I hop out of my car and jog up to the third floor.

I give the door three quick knocks. Hiding my hands behind my back, I wait for her to answer. Within moments, the door swings open.

Lena stands on the other side in a long black t-shirt down to her knees—one I don't recognize—her hair is tied up into a high, messy bun.

Her mouth falls open, and she takes a breath in.

"Good morning, babe." It doesn't go unnoticed how she hesitates in greeting me, and it doesn't go unnoticed how she hasn't invited me in yet. She doesn't smile when she sees me. Well, not the same kind of smile as last night. This one's fake, forced, and waning.

Her hand is still holding the door, but I step in anyway, passing her on my way, making sure to keep my hands held behind my back, ensuring she doesn't see what I'm holding.

Lena closes the door then turns around, staying in the entryway. She points to me. "What's behind your back?"

Slowly, I take a few steps forward. I'm still angry about last night, and I'm skeptical of this shirt she's wearing. It's definitely too big to be hers or any woman's, for that matter. Not to mention, it has a large fucking Boston Bruins logo on the front.

I quickly place a kiss on her lips and step back. I ignore her question and ask her mine instead, my eyes dancing along her half-naked body.

"New shirt?"

She immediately follows my gaze and looks down, grabbing the hem of her shirt. She lifts it as if she's looking at it for the first time as if she didn't realize she was wearing it.

"Oh..." she explains, waving me off. "This is just an old shirt my Uncle bought for me when he went to a game. I've had it since I was eleven."

28

She lets go of the shirt and looks back up to me.

I watch the fabric fall back against the smooth skin of her thighs. I don't believe a fucking word she said, but with the way she looks in that shirt and my hunger to be inside of her, I let it go —If only to give me enough time to be with her first before we get down to the bullshit.

"Julian," she says with a small grin. "What's behind your back?" She changes the subject and for once, I'm okay with it.

"You'll see," I wink and begin walking backward to her bedroom. I've been inside her apartment enough times to know where her room is without having to look.

Giggling, she follows me, her bare feet padding across the cool hardwood floor.

"Julian..."

Her voice travels through me. The warm morning sun peeks through her windows, highlighting her hair and smooth pale skin. I fight to control myself until I make it back to her bedroom.

"What?" I ask, teasing, stepping into her room.

"I want to know what's behind your back." She lunges forward, attempting to reach behind me. I step to the side, away from her.

Catching her mouth, I press mine against hers. She stops in front of me and places her hands on my shoulders.

"Julian," she whispers.

I press my lips to her neck, tasting her sweet morning skin. "Wrong name," I whisper back with a subtle nod of my head.

"Well, Mr. Price," she says. "I did tell you we would make up for last night."

"Yes, you did." Breaking my lips away from her neck, I step back. I nod toward her bed. "Lie down."

Arching an eyebrow, she hesitates. "Really?"

"Yeah," I say on a laugh, only half filled with humor, the other half dead fucking serious.

"Okay." She turns around with a smirk and crawls across her queen size bed.

She crawls across the mattress on her hands and knees and fuck me if it wasn't the sexiest thing I've ever seen in my life.

Her t-shirt rides up, and her bare ass is on full display. She's not wearing anything under that hideous Bruins shirt. Goddamn.

Stopping halfway, she turns her head and looks over her shoulder.

"Now, Mr. Price, are you going to show me what's behind your back?"

I wring my fingers on the silk fabric of the tie I'm still hiding behind me. I had every intention of coming over here and reminding Lena of who she belongs to. But now, I'm not so sure I can take it slow as I intended.

She eyes me, her gaze still hovering over her shoulder. I don't take my eyes off her hips and her round ass still facing me.

Finally, I move my arms and toss the tie to the floor. I can still show Lena she's mine without the tie.

Her eyes follow the tie, watching it as it flies across the room, landing in the corner by her hamper. The desire leaves her eyes only momentarily as she stares at the tie. Her mouth closes, and her neck dips.

I take a step toward the bed, grabbing the waist of my sweatpants.

"Something wrong?" I ask her. I take another step forward.

She's still on her hands and knees, her eyes still fixated on the stupid ass tie.

"No." She clears her throat. "Nothing."

Then with a subtle shake of her head, she finally turns back to me, looking back over her shoulder. "It's nothing." Her voice is quiet and careful.

She doesn't know what I'm going to do, and I like that. I'm keeping her guessing. Her eyes are filled with a sense of hesitation, and once I start stepping out of my sweatpants and freeing my cock, I'm ready.

I step up behind her, remove my shirt and toss it alongside the tie. Placing my hands on her hips, my fingers dig into the soft, supple flesh of her hips as I pull her toward me in one motion. Her knees slide against the mattress, and her ass pushes against me. I groan, feeling her so close.

Pushing up the back of her shirt, I slide it halfway up her back, exposing her lower half.

"You want to know why I brought the tie?"

Smoothing my hand over her round ass, I flick my eyes to hers, waiting for her answer. "Answer me."

She inhales a sharp breath. "Yes." Her voice quivers, and I jerk her hips against me, needing this. Needing her.

"I brought it because…" I reach around, sliding my hand along her stomach. When I find her warmth, I slip my fingers down, feeling her wetness. Her back arches, her ass pressing into me on her own volition now. "I brought it because I wanted to remind you of something."

My fingers circle her clit, her body already shivering beneath my touch. I can already tell she's losing her ability to resist, her ability to speak. She moans and bends down, pressing her face against the green silk sheets,

her ass raised as high as it will go. She spreads her arms out on the mattress, fisting the fabric as my circles grow faster and wider.

"Do you want to know what I came here to remind you of?"

Moaning, she turns her head, pressing her cheek deeper into the mattress, her eyes closed, and her mouth falls open.

I stop, my fingers resting on her hot, wanting skin. "I can't hear you, Lena. What did I come here to remind you of?"

Her eyes fall open, and her breaths are heavy. "Um, I'm not sure, Jul…. Mr. Price."

Pulling my hand from between her legs, I smooth both hands over her ass again. Her body shivers as I slide my hand between the back of her legs, spreading them.

Grabbing my cock, I position myself in front of her, at her entrance.

"I came here to remind you that you're mine." Pulling back, I push myself into Lena as hard and as fast as I can. "Mine."

A loud scream escapes her throat. I groan, feeling her warmth and wetness surrounding me. She feels fucking amazing. My head swims—it feels like I've taken some kind of drug, and I'm already flying fucking high.

I lose myself in Lena, and my thrusts become faster, claiming her as mine. Then as my body tingles, like fireworks bursting against my skin, I realize one thing. I came here with the intention of showing Lena how much she's mine using the tie now so carelessly discarded on the floor. Instead, all I needed to do was say a few words, bending her to do my bidding.

I didn't think I was going to be able to control myself in showing Lena how much she means to me. How so deep she is in this with me. But I guess I underestimated Lena's powers.

And I guess I underestimated how she gives me the power to do things I didn't even know I was capable of.

FOUR

"What time are you meeting her?"

"Um," Lena looks down at her phone, checking the time. "In about fifteen minutes." She's standing in front of the mirror in her bathroom, applying a thin layer of red lipstick.

"You don't need to wear lipstick if you're meeting her for lunch, do you? It's too much if you ask me."

Her hand stops, hovering in front of her lip. She's staring at me through the reflection of the mirror. "I didn't ask—"

When I narrow my eyes at her reflection with my arms crossed over my chest, she stops, rethinking her words. She reaches over the counter and pulls out a makeup wipe.

"You're right. It is too much."

I kiss the top of her head, and her eyes meet mine in the mirror. "Good," I say. She's nearly wiped all of it away when I add, "Much better."

Leaving her in the bathroom, I walk over to where I discarded my shirt and tie earlier. I put my shirt back on and begin neatly folding the tie. Feeling the silk fabric sliding between my fingers, I grin.

"Where are you meeting Abby?"

When I turn around, Lena is standing inside of her closet, searching through her shirts.

"She wanted to go to the Coffee Trade."

"Really?"

She chooses a black, V-neck t-shirt and a grey cardigan. Her light-wash, torn jeans hug her legs like they were made for her. She walks out of her closet and sits at the end of her bed, putting her shoes on. After sliding one shoe on, she looks up to me and.

"Yep. That's where Abby wanted to go, so that's where we're going."

I clear my throat. My hands shiver with the lingering memory of Lena's skin against mine. My cock pulses, remembering how she feels, how it feels to be inside her. She didn't fight against me this morning. She was ready and willing, so I decide to let this one slide. Her choice in outfit doesn't even bother me.

"Okay. Well, make sure to come by my place afterward." Lena's still sitting on the edge of her bed. Standing in front of her, I cup her face with my hands, tilting her head up to me. Her head is right in line with my waist and sliding my hands against her cheeks, I thread my fingers through her hair, pushing it back.

A weak smile spreads across her mouth. "I can't."

A breath escapes me. My fingers are still laced through the strands of her blond hair, feeling them slide against my skin as I press my fingertips into her head. I clench my jaw and hold my breath.

"Why not?"

"Abby." She swallows. "Abby and I might do something afterward."

I loosen my hands around her head and let her slip away. I back away, standing in the middle of her room.

"Listen, Julian." She slaps her hands on her knees with a sigh. ""Listen, Julian. I know what you're thinking. I know you don't like Abby, but she's my friend." She stands up and leaves the room, walking toward the front of her apartment. I follow, tie still in hand. "I promised Abby I would make up for last night," she adds. "We might go see a movie or something."

Lena won't look me in the eye, searching the countertops of her kitchen. For what, I have no fucking clue. All I know is, she refuses to look me in the eye since we moved to the living room.

I clench my jaw even tighter than earlier. At this rate, I'm going to lose half my teeth.

"Fine." I grab onto her elbow, stopping her. We're standing in the entryway with me on the side of the front door. She can't leave without passing me first.

She looks at my hand, and this time I know I've caught her attention. Finally, her eyes move from where my hand is wrapped around her elbow to me. She stares into my eyes, but no words leave her mouth.

I smirk. "Have fun with Abby."

Her breaths suddenly grow heavier. I didn't mean a fucking word—not one single fucking word—and she knows it. The difference between Lena and me is I don't give a shit whether she has fun with Abby. I just want her to come back to me. I want to be the only person in her life.

Bending my knees, I lean in and kiss her, keeping my hand wrapped around her arm, showing her how much I love her. Then I release her elbow and walk out the door, clenching my tie in my hand.

RUNNING DOWN THE STAIRS, THE ANGER FROM LEAVING LENA STILL courses through me. Why must she make everything so fucking difficult? My mother was the same way. My father was the same way.

Everything had to be difficult. Everything was a struggle. And I swore I would never be with a woman like my mother.

When I make it to my car, I slam both hands down on the trunk, then pace the sidewalk, thinking about what I'm going to do. Even after the incredible sex I had with Lena this morning, I still feel like something's wrong. She's acting strange, and I can't put my finger on it.

Making sure I'm gone before Lena comes outside, I jump in my car and leave the parking lot, driving in the direction of the Coffee Trade. When I'm in the vicinity of the coffee shop, I don't park close. I find an apartment building a block away and park behind it, making sure my car is surrounded by others. Parked in between two large pickup trucks, my heart thrashes inside my chest.

I think about how I'm going to do this. I need to be careful. I need to make sure neither Lena nor Abby see me.

Before I step out of my car, I search my car for something I could use to disguise myself. I didn't even bother thinking to change my clothes. I'm a mess. I look like a fucking idiot, going to a coffee shop dressed like I'm going to the gym. But I don't think on it too long, driven by my desire to find out what's going on with Lena. I find a hat I discarded on the floorboard behind the passenger seat. Situating it on my head, I glance in the rearview mirror. It's a Brown University baseball cap, one with the crest stitched right on the front. Lena bought it for me when we had gone to the gift shop, and I told her how atrocious it was, wondering why anyone in their right mind would wear such a thing. The moment she gave it to me, I tossed it in the backseat, allowing it to be forgotten… until now.

Satisfied, I step out of my car, ready to head over to the coffee shop. Shoving my hands into the pockets of my sweatpants, I walk quickly, unsure how far ahead of Lena I am.

Passing by the shops, I try to pick up my steps. I want to make sure I get to the Coffee Trade before Lena, but I need to make sure Abby doesn't see me. I'm sure she's already there, waiting and reserving a table for them, something Abby would do. She's controlling and obsessive about Lena.

The street is lined with various local shops and restaurants. Being only a few blocks from the University, this part of Providence is very popular as far as student hangouts go. Today is especially busy. It's springtime in the North, and it's a Saturday. I lucked out.

I blend in with the constant stream of students and tourists walking the streets. The closer I grow to the coffee shop, the slower my steps become. I finally spot it at the end of the street. Even if I've only been here a handful of times, I can still easily recognize it. The Coffee Trade was often the place Lena and I would have our group study sessions for our Art History class. The building is painted a vivid white, a dark blue sign, "The Coffee Trade," hanging above. It fits right in with the whole New England theme. Edging closer to the buildings, I walk alongside them, peering through their windows as if I'm just another student, another tourist.

I glance over my shoulder on both sides, making sure I don't see Lena or Abby. When I'm confident the street is only filled with strangers, I walk up to the front of the coffee shop, edging up to the window. My hands still buried deep into my pockets, I flex my fingers, gripping the fabric and hold my breath.

From the very edge of the window, I peek through and scan the tables for Abby.

Above the ordering counter, black chalkboard menus line the walls. Three baristas furiously walk back and forth between the cash register and espresso machines. Every one of them is young, most likely students working to pay their way through college. Luckily, I didn't have to stoop to their level. If there's one thing my parents did right, it's they didn't make shit for money. So, when it came time for me to apply for financial aid, scholarships, and grants, I was a shoe-in. I was given more money than I knew what to do with. Well, actually it's the reason I was able to afford the things I have, such as my car and my perfectly tailored suits. I look down at my clothes once again in disappointment and frustration. Shit, I hate looking like shit.

Shaking my head, I return to the task at hand. I'm watching the baristas, taking orders and making shit lattes and cappuccinos for the constant flow of customers, when I spot Abby. I sigh with relief when I see her standing in line, her back to me. She's unmistakable. Her long silver hair lies against her back perfectly, shining against the sunlight filtering in through the window. I don't immediately walk in. I wait until she's ordered her coffee and carries her drink over to a small table near the back.

When I'm positive she won't see me, I walk into the coffee shop. Of course, I don't order a thing. It's not part of my plan. The table Abby chose is secluded and separated by a bookshelf, dividing the back section of the dining room from the rest of the tables. She's sitting on a bench lining the wall. The bookshelf being used as a divider isn't completely stocked, so I'm nervous, wondering if I'll be able to pull this off.

I quickly make my way to the back of the restaurant. When I find a table close enough to Abby, I sit down on the booth and slide across until I'm right next to hers, on the other side of the bookshelf. I pick up a menu, using it to block my face and tip my head down, covering my eyes for when Lena walks by. I can't risk her seeing me.

I set my phone down on the table, behind the menu. It's been exactly fifteen minutes since I left Lena at her apartment, standing there in her entryway. She's supposed to have been here by now, but I'm not surprised when she finally shows up two minutes later. She's even late for Abby. What the fuck?

"Abby!" Lena's voice travels in front of me.

Hearing her, I peek over the top of my menu, careful not to let my green eyes show too much. I leave just enough space between the top of my hat and the menu to see what's going on. Abby slides along the booth beside me, on the opposite side of the bookshelf. She stands and meets Lena who is now directly in front of my table.

Lena wraps her arms around Abby, resting her chin on her shoulder. She looks just as she did when I left her standing there in her apartment.

"Lena, I've missed you," Abby coos. She sounds like a twelve-year-old girl on the first day of school, the one who hasn't seen her best friend all summer. She's acting as if she hasn't seen Lena in the last week. But I know she has. Abby is just being dramatic as always.

"I've missed you too, sweets." Lena releases her hold on Abby, and they both sit down at the table Abby originally saved. They didn't notice me, they didn't even bother glancing in my direction. Thank God.

The bookshelf dividing us is full of books of all kinds. Mostly, they're the ones you find in antique stores. The covers are woven, the scent of aged paper mingling with freshly roasted coffee. I peek through the small cracks above the books. If It weren't for this gigantic, floor to ceiling bookshelf, I would be sitting catty-corner from Lena.

I'm able to keep my head tipped low and peer at Lena without her seeing me. The hairs on the back of my neck stand on end and chills run through my body. I'm here, she's here.

I hold my breath, watching and listening.

"Abby," Lena groans. She pushes the sleeves of her cardigan up her forearms, resting her elbows on the table. "I'm so sorry I had to ditch you last night."

"I know," Abby sighs, reaching across the table grabbing Lena's hand. "I'm just worried about you. I want you to be okay."

"Yeah." Lena's bottom lip quivers as she inhales a shaky breath.

I rest my arm on the table and clench my fist, my nails digging into the palm of my hand.

Why would Abby be worried if Lena was okay? Of course, she's fucking okay. And with the incredible fuck we had this morning, she should be still be riding the high that comes with having sex with me.

"*Are* you okay?" Abby asks.

Lena looks down at her hands, still holding onto Abby's. "Not really..." Her voice drifts off as my heart rate picks up.

I feel like I'm sliding off the edge of a cliff. My heart picks up, but my stomach flips at the same time. It's as if someone has pushed me off a cliff before I've even had the opportunity to ask why.

Lena's eyes tear up as she breathes in. Her eyes dart to the right, away from me. I'm thankful because I'm afraid if she even glances in this direction, she might see me. Or even get the inkling I'm here.

Lena swipes her cheek, using her fingers to soak up her tears.

"You haven't talked to him yet, have you, Lena?" Abby asks.

"No," Lena says, disappointed.

I close my eyes wondering who Abby is talking about. All I know is, it isn't me because Lena tells me everything. She doesn't keep secrets from me. And she's happy with me. With *me*.

"Lena, you have to do it soon. You can't keep living like this."

"I know." Lena sniffs as she nods. I can tell she and Abby have had a conversation similar to this one. I can tell because Lena avoids making eye contact with Abby, tilting her head to the side and looks down at the table.

I swear, this is the most fucking depressing lunch I've ever been a part of. Well, more like been a witness to. Abby is being a whiny bitch, making Lena cry and cower. I would never do this to her. So, why Lena was insistent on this lunch is beyond me.

Also, I can't help but wonder who Abby is talking about. Who does Lena still need to speak to?

Lena's eyes move from the table to the bookshelf. She lingers there for longer than expected, her eyes drifting off in thought.

The air gets lodged in my throat as I lean back, immediately looking down at the table. I don't know if Lena caught my gaze, or if she could even see me through the many cracks and spaces between the books. Suddenly, I start coughing, the sting of the air being lodged in my throat catching up with me.

I raise my clenched fist in front of my mouth, attempting to rid myself of the coughing fit. I don't need this right now. I don't fucking need this.

I'm making a scene. I'm bent over, resting my arm on the table when I see a person stand in front of my table.

At first, I'm afraid it's Lena or Abby, but the bottom of a black apron catches my eye. I look up to find one of the baristas, a small brunette woman, standing in front of me, her hands clasped in front of her.

"Are you okay, sir?"

I swallow, my coughs slowing down. The room is quiet except for the subtle coffeehouse music playing overhead. Abby isn't talking anymore, and neither is Lena. Panicked, I take a chance and peek through the bookshelf again. They've both turned their heads toward the bookshelf, in my direction, obviously knowing something is going on.

I shift in my booth, afraid they've already seen me. What if Lena saw my hat? What if she could sense it was me by my coughs?

My palms sweat and I cough one more time when the barista asks again, "Sir, can I get you anything? A glass of water maybe?"

Snapping my head up, I keep my back toward Lena and Abby's table. I narrow my eyes, annoyed with the young woman standing before me. She's only drawing more attention to me, making this whole situation worse.

Giving her a warning look, I vehemently shake my head.

Inhaling a deep breath, I finally gain control of myself. I want to tell the barista to fuck off, to mind her own business, but I can't.

Instead, I shake my head once more before the stupid, obnoxious woman rolls her eyes and stalks back to the checkout counter with a huff.

It doesn't take long before Lena and Abby start talking again. I hold my breath, worried they know but convince myself they haven't. I didn't talk, and they haven't seen me. If Lena had, she would have said something.

Fuck. That was close.

"Lena, you *need* to do it. And soon."

I keep my back to the bookshelf. I can't risk any more chances, so I stay still. My back is rigid, and my arms are flexed. I just need to stay long enough to know who Abby keeps talking about.

"I know," Lena sighs. "I just needed to get through the rest of classes, which I've done. Then graduation, which is literally right around the corner. Actually, I talked to him about the showing at the Museum in Boston. I'm going to do it then. I just need to make sure I'm doing it at the right time. I need to make sure I'm careful." She pauses. "You know how he gets."

My head starts to pound and the room spins. I realize it's because I've tightened and flexed my jaw so hard, I've brought on an indescribable amount of pain to myself. My teeth grate against one another, the pain shooting through the nerves in my gums.

Clenching my fist even tighter, my nails dig into my palm once again. When I unclench my fist, relieving myself of the pain, I look down at my hand. A small amount of blood lines my fingernails, small crescent shaped indentations etched into the skin of my palm.

"Let me go with you," Abby says. "I can make sure you're okay afterward. You don't even have to talk to me or anything like that. You can pretend you don't know I'm there."

"No," Lena replies. Her voice is strained, almost as if she's not so sure. Her words hold no conviction. "I'll be fine, Abby. I know how to handle Julian. Besides, we'll be at the museum so it's not like he can hurt me. You know how he likes to keep up his image. He won't risk it in front of a bunch of prestigious artists. He won't tarnish his reputation."

Fire engulfs my throat, my eyes sting, and my skin burns with anger. I struggle to keep myself together, to not draw attention to myself, but the raging fire in me is nearly becoming too much for me to bear. I swallow the fire, putting it out long enough to hear a bit more. All I need is a little more.

"There's one other thing." Lena's voice slows, drawing out each word, but this time, her words are a bit lighter. "You don't have to worry about what happens with Julian in Boston because Logan will be there. He said he'd make sure I make it back here, back home, safely."

"Logan, huh?" Abby takes a sip of her coffee. "I thought you two were just friends."

"We were, we were," Lena grins, staring at her hands. "I didn't intend on growing feelings for Logan. But he listens to me, and he isn't controlling like Julian is. He makes me feel like I'm more than just a piece of ass."

"Have you told Logan how you feel about him yet?"

"No, not yet," Lena sighs, her eyes taking on a tremendous amount of sadness. "I know I need to let go of Julian before fully moving on with Logan. I just can't help the way I feel."

"That's great, Lena," Abby coos. "Trust me, you'll be so much happier when..."

I slam my fist on the table, unwilling to listen to the rest of Abby's sentence. I can't take it anymore. The salt and pepper shakers jump off the table and topple over, sprinkling across the table in one motion.

A few people stop mid-conversation, their heads turn my way as they look at me with either questioning faces or ones of anger like I've somehow disturbed their precious coffee drinking.

Fuckers. All of them.

Shoving my hands into the deep pockets of my sweatpants, I storm out of the coffee shop before anyone has a chance to recognize me.

By the time I make it to the parking lot behind the apartment building down the street, I realize Lena spoke a name I've heard before.

One fucking name.

Logan.

FIVE

I've always preferred the taste of red wine to whiskey.

The first time I ever tasted whiskey was when I was ten. My father used to leave an open bottle on the table in the living room of our trailer. As always, beside the bottle was his favorite whiskey glass, the letters 'CP' engraved on the side.

The first memory I have of whiskey is also the same memory I have of the first time I *tasted* whiskey.

After school was my favorite part of the day. It was the only hour where I was able to be in our trailer by myself. I would storm in through the front door, allowing the screen door to slam back, the kitchen being my first stop.

I'd fill my favorite blue plastic cup to the top with milk then carefully carry it to the living room to watch my favorite afternoon cartoons.

I had one hour. One hour where I knew I could actually be a kid. I could lie on the couch, resting my chin on the arm with my legs bent, wagging them in the air, and not have to focus on anything but a cat chasing a mouse or if the coyote would catch the roadrunner.

Then as the hour ticked by, I knew my father would come home from work soon. He'd make his first glass of whiskey. He would come into our trailer, trashed, the whiskey already soaked so far into his veins, it was seeping out of his pores.

That day, the coyote had just been crushed by an anvil when my father stumbled through the screen door as expected.

I scrambled, snatching up the remote to turn off the TV, and sat up. But as I was sitting up, my foot swung over the small worn-down coffee table, spilling the milk. The white liquid splashed across the table, dripping down into the musty, forest green carpet.

"Julian!"

My breath caught in my throat as my head snapped up. My father stood directly in front of me, his eyes piercing and on fire.

Quickly standing up, I tried to run the five-foot distance to the kitchen but didn't make it two feet before I felt my father's hand grip my shirt. He then wrapped his hand around the back of my neck, his fingers digging in. My body went stiff, my back rigid, feeling the pain shoot straight to my toes.

"What the fuck do you think you're doing, boy?" he yelled, forcing me to turn back around to the spilled milk. "You make this place look like shit!"

"I'm sorry, Daddy." My feet shuffled across the carpet as he took me back to the spilled milk, then used his hand to shove me. I fell onto the couch in one fell swoop. Biting my tongue, I fought back the tears, knowing how much my father hated it.

Swaying back and forth, he practically danced over to his half-empty bottle of whiskey. "Julian, my boy," he slurred. "Listen carefully." With hooded eyes, he glanced at me, pouring the caramel-colored liquor into his favorite glass, just like I had with the milk. He filled it to the top as I sank farther into the couch. I wanted to get away from him. I wanted to rewind back to an hour before—to a time when I was just another ten-year-old watching afterschool cartoons.

I didn't answer him. I waited and listened carefully, just as he asked.

"Julian." He took a large gulp of his drink, stumbling his way over to me. "There's one important thing you need to remember in life." The couch sank beside me as he sat down, leaning toward me,

the whiskey sloshing and spilled out of his glass as he held it out to me. "There's only one thing in life you need to remember," he said. "And that's to never apologize for anything. Ever."

Pressing my lips together, I swallowed and stared up at him with wide, fearful eyes. "Yes, Daddy. I understand."

"Good," he grinned. "Now, be a man and take a drink."

"Good evening, sir. What can I get you?"

My eyes move from the bartender standing in front of me to the shelf behind him.

About a hundred types of liquor bottles are illuminated by different colored lights underneath them. I stare them down, my eyes darting from one label to the next.

"Sir?" the bartender asks.

Slowly, I look back over to him. "A whiskey. Straight up."

"Any specific kind?"

I laugh, but there's no humor behind it. "No."

"You got it." With a simple nod, he turns around, grabbing a bottle off the shelf.

I'm resting my forearms on the edge of the bar counter in Bar Americano. My impulse to keep looking over my shoulders has been eating away at me since the moment I sat down. I came here to see him. I needed to know whether what I heard was true. Did Lena really know this man? Was he more to her than a simple fucking goofy-ass waiter who served us last night?

Honestly, I'm not quite sure what I'm even looking for. The asshole is just a fucking waiter. I'm sure there isn't much to discover about him. I wasn't even sure if he was here. But I need to know. Which brings me to where I am now, at the bar ordering a fucking whiskey.

The bartender places a small white square napkin in front of me followed by a glass of whiskey. I smirk, knowing it's not even half as full as what my father used to pour in his glass. Bartender's a little stingy with the alcohol, I see.

I stare at my glass, twisting it around in my hand before I even bring it up to my lips. I imagine the letters, CP, that were engraved on my father's glass. I imagine them being etched into the glass I'm now holding, how it would look if it were a JP instead.

But I know that glass was buried a long time ago along with my father's cold, lifeless body, at my mother's insistence.

Lifting the glass, I bring it to my lips. The scent overwhelms me, and my first reaction is to gag. My throat seizes at the smell, but I swallow it down, unwilling to let the feeling overpower me.

WITHOUT ANOTHER MOMENT OF HESITATION, I TAKE ONE LONG, slow sip.

The malted liquid glides across my tongue, my taste buds igniting. It's warm, and as it makes its way down my throat and into the pit of my stomach, a familiar feeling overwhelms me.

I bring the glass back to my mouth, finishing off the rest. I slam it on the counter and call the bartender back over.

"I'd like another one. This time make it a double."

"Yes, sir."

When he turns around and begins making my second drink, I look over my right shoulder.

I'm facing away from the entrance to the kitchen. The bar is located in the center of the restaurant, basically making one giant circle in the middle of the dining room. I'm scanning the room for Logan, hoping to catch him emerging from the kitchen at some point. Or at least before the whiskey starts to take effect.

But I can't wait to see Logan. The bartender doesn't even get the chance to place my drink down in front of me before I swipe it from his hand, immediately drinking half of it. I ignore the way he scoffs and raises his eyebrows.

He can go fuck off.

Twenty minutes later, I'm on my third glass of whiskey when I finally see Logan. The kitchen door swings open as he and another waiter emerge.

He's dressed the same as he was last night. White button-up shirt tucked into black dress pants. Only now, he's carrying his black apron in his arm, wrapped around his server book. He looks like an asshole—everything from his long brown hair tied back into a bun to the light scruff lining his jaw. He looks like he crawled out of the dumpster from behind the restaurant.

Breaking away from watching him, I turn my attention back to the bar, hoping the bartender has refilled my drink without having to ask again.

I grin when I see the caramel-colored liquid patiently waiting for me. Throwing the drink back, my throat growing numb to the usual burn, I finish it in one gulp, just as my phone vibrates on the bar counter.

I loosen the tie around my neck, watching my phone move across the glazed wood. After I left the coffee shop, I stopped by my apartment to shower and change into a fresh suit. It felt wrong to stay in sweatpants, and I knew I needed to get out and do something to take my mind off Lena and her shit secrets. Logan was the first thing that came to mind.

Lena's name flashes across the screen of my phone just as I feel the whiskey burning in my bloodstream. It feels as if the whiskey has now become a part of me, consuming me.

Smirking, I finally pick up my phone. Pressing it to my ear, I swing around in my barstool, resting my back against the bar. I rest my arm back onto the counter, scanning the dining room for Logan again.

I find him standing near the host stand, chatting with two other waiters. I don't understand him. Why is he always laughing and smiling? It makes no fucking sense. And how could he possibly be so happy when he looks the way he does and works a shit job?

"Hey, babe." My tongue stings with the words. I'm playing with Lena, and the very thought of knowing her secrets excites me. I'm no longer bitter about her keeping them from me. I'm excited, thrilled to be able to play this game with her.

"Hello, baby." She sounds happy, the tone of her voice a contradiction to the fear she had in the coffee shop. To be honest, I'm the last person Lena should be afraid of, and I'll set out to prove it. "How was your day?"

I want to laugh, but I hold myself back. My eyes narrow in on Logan. He hasn't moved, and if I didn't know any better, I notice his attention wavers in the direction of the bar from time to time.

"It was good, Lena," I answer. "Didn't do much. How was your lunch with Abby?"

She pauses, and although she can't see me, I can't help but smile. Her hesitation thrills me, especially with my eyes locked on an equally oblivious fucker like Logan. It's fun being the one who knows everything.

"It was so good to see her," she sighs. "I've missed her."

Swirling back around in my seat, I pick up my glass and tilt it back. I swallow the one or two drops left, unsure whether I want to order another—not because I couldn't use another one, I really fucking could—but because I need to keep an eye on Logan, ready to move when he does.

"I know you have," is all I say. Even whiskey won't allow me to be thrown into a conversation about how my girlfriend misses her best friend. I don't elaborate, hoping we can move on from the topic of Abby. I erase the vision of her and Lena together at the coffee shop, her hand reaching across the table, comforting Lena in her sadness.

I don't for one second believe the bullshit plan Lena had relayed to Abby. And I don't for one second believe Lena is unhappy. I just need to figure out how Logan fits into all of this.

"Well..." Lena's voice drifts off. I can tell she's thinking of what to say, plotting her next words.

"Would you like me to come over now?" I'm testing her. The whiskey, still blatantly present in my body and flowing through my veins, is screaming the obvious answer at me. I know what she's going to say, I just need to hear her say it. I need her to prove me right.

"Um," she yawns. "Actually, babe, I'm pretty tired. Abby and I went and saw a movie after lunch, and I'm beat. I think I'm just going to go to bed. Why don't I call you tomorrow?"

My eyes follow Logan as he makes his way toward the front door of the restaurant. I keep Lena on the phone as I slide off my barstool, slapping a one hundred-dollar bill down on the counter next to my empty glass. The bartender never gave me my check, but I don't give a fuck.

"Fine." I tighten my jaw, clenching my teeth together. It's as if it's my body's automatic response to Lena now. Gripping my phone, I press it against my cheek. "I'll call you in the morning."

"Okay. I love you, Julian."

Keeping my eyes on Logan, I leave the bar and weave in between the tables, following him.

"Goodnight, Lena."

After hanging up, I push open the large glass door, feeling the cool night air flash against my face. The ground is still wet from the earlier rainfall, and my black shoes tap against the soaked concrete. I avoid the obvious puddles, not wanting to make much noise.

I stop where the sidewalk meets the parking lot, waiting to see where Logan goes. Headlights blink as he unlocks his beat up Honda Civic. What a joke.

I'm not surprised. Not at all.

The valet pulls my car up, just as Logan starts up his shit car and drives out of the parking lot. I snatch the keys out of the valet's hand without tipping him. As I sit in the driver's seat and press my foot down on the gas pedal, it's as if the whiskey is finally waking up, burning every part of my body—m

y head spins, my skin tingles, my hands grip onto the steering wheel. The night is crisp and clear, giving me the perfect view of Logan. My engine roars and my heart races.

There's something about Logan. And there's something about

the way Lena talked about him at her lunch with Abby. I wish I could say I was wrong. That all of my instincts are telling me that I'm making a bigger deal of this than it really is.

But the other part of me, the one my father instilled into me at a young age, tells me otherwise. Not all women are loyal. And as my father believed, you could never fully trust a woman.

It isn't hard to follow Logan. Mostly because I recognize the neighborhood he's driving through.

A car pulls out in front of me, putting space between me and Logan. Normally, I might be worried, but I'm not. I know these streets, mostly because I drive them every day.

Logan's shit red car turns right, and my stomach dips. The whiskey erupts, searing its way into the back of my throat.

"You fucking asshole," I mutter as Logan pulls into the parking lot of Lena's apartment complex. I stay far back, hidden behind a row of cars. I turn my headlights off, preparing myself for what I'm about to see. "You fucking asshole."

Seconds after pulling up, Logan steps out of his car. He leans against the side of it, the engine still rattling. He doesn't wait for long before he grins at Lena coming down the steps.

She's dressed in her torn black jeans, the same ones she was wearing for me the other day. Only this time, she's wearing a blue Boston t-shirt.

My hand hovers over the handle of my door. A heavy weight bears down on me, keeping me glued to my seat. I fight, pulling and urging myself to get out of the car. I imagine the feeling when my knuckles meet Logan's jaw. I imagine the way my chest would feel, sparking to life, knowing I had taken control.

Because when Lena grins as she practically runs down the stairs and wraps her arms around Logan's shoulders, I bite back the temptation. I bite back the desire to beat the shit out of the man leaning in to kiss my girlfriend outside of his piece of shit car.

SIX

I've gone back and forth all week, rethinking my decision to go to Boston with Lena. Well, in reality, I only questioned it one time. I'm smarter than that. I may be questioning what's going on in Lena's head, but I haven't let it cloud my judgment when it comes to bolstering my career.

Doubt had crossed my mind only the once, knowing I could potentially be losing Lena that night. But my desire to launch my career and become the artist I knew I would be clearly overshadowed that minor detail. Because let's be real, she isn't leaving me.

Syrup drips from my fork as I pick up another bite of French toast. I shove the soft, sweet bread into my mouth and stare at Lena across the table.

"Okay," she says with a smile. She's been oddly happy lately. Everything she says is either followed up with a smile or a laugh. Not to mention, she hasn't argued or fought against any of my decisions.

Take Monday for instance. I wanted to go see a movie at seventy-thirty. She not only agreed, but she showed up at seven on the dot, just like I asked—not a minute, or two, late.

Then on Tuesday, I showed up at her door unexpectedly, silk tie in hand. Her grin was ever present, true and genuine. That night, I wrapped the tie around her wrists, tying her to the metal bed frame of her bed. I fucked her, right there, in every position I could think of. With all the strength I could conjure up, I gripped her hips, my fingers digging into her soft, supple flesh and filled her completely, reminding her how much I love her.

I kept my knowledge about Logan a secret, letting the chips fall where they may. If that happened to be at the exhibit in Boston, then so be it. I knew what I needed to do for the outcome to fall my way. I knew how to hold up my perfect reputation as Lena liked to call it.

"Oh my God, babe. You have to try these crepes." Lena stabs a forkful of her strawberry cheesecake crepe and holds it out to me.

I narrow my eyes, curling the corner of my mouth into a smirk. Dropping my jaw without another word, I open my mouth, waiting for her to feed it to me.

Staying true to her shift in mood this week, she takes my hint and leans over the table, happy to oblige.

I close my mouth over her fork before she pulls it away with a giggle. Her eyes shine, reflecting against the warm, shining sun. We're sitting on the patio of a small café on the outskirts of Providence.

It's a nice, warm, mid-morning brunch, one Lena didn't protest to. I sit back in my metal chair and look at her. Her blonde hair is tied high into a bun, just the way I like it, tiny, random strands falling loosely around her slim and delicate face. They float against the smooth skin of her cheeks with the occasional breeze blowing across the patio. I tilt my chin up, enjoying the moment. A familiar feeling washes over me, one I felt when Lena was first mine.

She's fucking gorgeous, and the pride I feel for having her is almost more than I think I can take. The feeling warms me as she lifts her napkin, wiping the corner of her mouth. My eyes laser focus on her lips, remembering how they were wrapped around my cock just this morning, giving me the best blow job of my life.

My cock throbs beneath the fabric of my pants. Fuck, I wish we were somewhere less... public.

"Are you ready for graduation next week?"

I watch Lena's lips move with every word, still thinking about her this morning—her jaw slack, her body thrumming with the orgasm I gave her.

"Julian?"

The sound of Lena's voice growing louder rips my eyes away from her mouth and up to her eyes.

"Hmm?"

"Did you," she clears her throat. "Are you ready for graduation next week?" She finishes chewing the last bit of her crepe and takes a sip of her mimosa.

"Yes," I tell her. "Of course, I am. Are you?"

"I am. I ordered my cap and gown a while back."

"That's great." I cross my arms and lean forward, resting them on the edge of the table. "I'm more excited about this exhibit in Boston. Maybe we'll be able to make some important business connections. You know, help us decide where we want to go after this."

Lena looks down at her plate, using the tip of her fork to push around a small piece of leftover strawberry.

"Um," she starts absently. "what kind of places were you thinking of going?"

"Anywhere, really," I shrug. "Los Angeles, Dallas, New York. Anywhere that has the most prestigious collection of art museums.

She looks up from her plate, resting her fork on the edge. She rests her chin the palm of her hand as her eyes search my face. "We?"

"Yes," I drag the word out, unsure of what she means. "It doesn't matter where I end up. You're following me wherever I go." I tilt my head. "I thought you already knew that."

She blinks several times then quickly shakes her head.

"No, you're right. I'm sorry." She squeezes her eyes shut then opens them wide, staring at me. "I don't know what I was thinking." A small laugh escapes her when she inhales a deep breath. "I'll be right back. I just have to use the restroom."

Twisting my mouth, I bite the side of my tongue, feeling the sharp point of my incisor pierce my flesh. My heart sinks, and the blood drains from my face.

There she is. There's the fake Lena, the one whose eyes can't seem to meet mine when she speaks.

She slides out from her chair and walks inside the café, leaving me by myself at our small table and with the last bit of French toast I have left.

I stare at the door Lena just walked through. "Fucking bull-shit!" I release a hot breath and follow it up with a pounding fist on the small table. The silverware clanks against the plates, the fork tumbling off the table onto the ground.

The others sitting around me, turn their heads, pinning me with scowls.

Looking around, I stare at all their stupid, ridiculous faces.

"What? Can I fucking help you?"

With hushed mumbles and shakes of their heads, they all look back down at their fucking croissants and fresh whipped butter.

A deep pressure builds behind my eyes. I pinch the bridge of my nose and take a deep breath. The table underneath my elbow shakes with a quiet vibration.

I open my eyes and find Lena's phone sitting beside her plate. The screen lights up, vibrating again.

Glancing around the patio and taking a peek through the door, I make sure no one is watching me, or Lena isn't coming. Reaching my arm across the table, I quickly pick up her phone.

I stare at the screen as Logan's name is displayed indicating he's sent two text messages. Why would she leave her phone?

My shaking thumb hovers over Lena's phone. I know her password. I've seen her enter it on more than one occasion, looking over her shoulder.

0824. Her birthday.

Immediately going to her thread of texts with Logan, I zero in on the most recent ones, the ones that alerted me to pick up Lena's phone in the first place.

My hand tightens around her phone as my eyes frantically read the words in bold type.

Logan: I know it's hard.

Logan: Hang in there. Only a couple more weeks, then we're free.

I fight the impulse to throw Lena's phone out into the street, leaving it to be run over by a speeding car.

Instead, I scroll back through the entire thread, reading texts dating back months. Lena's known Logan for longer than I thought.

My finger stops when I nearly scroll by a picture of Lena, dated a couple of days ago. She's standing in front of a mirror. I recognize it as the large, full-length one she has leaning against the wall in her bedroom. I've memorized that same mirror, having watched the reflection of me fucking Lena numerous times before. But in this picture, she's standing in front of it, wearing the same oversized Boston Bruins shirt I caught her wearing the first day I showed up to her apartment.

Her legs are bare, the shirt seemingly the only thing she's wearing. Below the picture, Logan's typed out a message.

Logan: You look sexy as hell wearing my shirt.

Pressing my lips together, I swallow what feels like hot coals burning down my throat and into my gut. My vision blurs, the image of Lena wearing Logan's shirt searing itself into my brain. She lied to me. The fucking whore *lied* to me.

My head spins as I toss Lena's phone back onto the table. I clench my fists once again, feeling my fingernails cutting into my skin. It's amazing how I've grown accustomed to the routine of pain I've inflicted on myself due to Lena's indiscretions.

I rake my fingers through my hair, pushing it back with a heavy-weighted breath. I'm not sure what I'm going to do. All I know is, I knew I was right as always. Something was off about that shirt, and Logan just fucking proved it.

I glance up when Lena comes back and sits down, a grin is plastered on her face, and if I didn't know any better, her eyes are slightly swollen from previously shed tears. Remnants of them ghost along her skin, the moisture glistening against the still rising sun.

"Are you okay, baby?" she asks.

I stare at Lena with narrowed eyes. I stare at her, wondering what I'm going to do. I feel helpless, at a loss for how to regain control of my relationship.

I've always felt like I've had a handle on my relationship with Lena. I never had to question where we were going or if she was going to go with me. I've lost control, and I don't like the feeling. In fact, I fucking despise it. And I know the only reason I'm feeling this way is because of Logan. Fucking Logan and his fucking Boston Bruins t-shirt. Who the fuck watches hockey, anyway?

Pretentious, girlfriend-stealing assholes, that's who.

"I'm fine." I toss my napkin onto my plate and wave our waiter down, indicating I'm ready for the check.

Several minutes pass in utter silence. I'm still staring at Lena, deep into her eyes. I have no fucking clue who she is anymore.

I'm even more confused when she suddenly stands.

"I'm sorry, baby, but I need to head out if I'm going to make it in time for that hot yoga class."

As if I've suddenly been awakened, I look up at Lena with a grin. I feel alive, the idea of how to handle this Logan situation breathing new life into me.

"You know," I start, lacing my voice with humor, distracting her, playing it off as if I have no fucking clue what's really going on. "I don't understand how anyone would *want* to take a hot yoga class. Don't you sweat enough in regular yoga?"

Lena laughs, leaning down and planting a kiss on my cheek. She quickly stands back up-right, bouncing on the heels of her workout shoes. Her black leggings stretch across her legs, her ass round and tight. I place my hand on her hip, pressing my thumb into her hip bone.

"I love it," she says. "It's more invigorating and refreshing when they pump the room full of steam. Relieves a lot of stress."

"What are you trying to say, Lena? That I stress you out?"

I meant the question to be a joke, one where I'm playing off our relationship as if we're the perfect fucking couple. But Lena's eyes dim, and her smile falters, fading with the light in her eyes. Just as it has a million times before, she plays off her reactions like I won't notice them. Like I'm not the same man she's been with for two years.

I can see her struggle to rebuild her smile.

"Of course, you don't Julian. I just mean life, in general, is stressful."

She starts to back away, heading toward the gate leading to the street. The patio is enclosed by a short metal fence.

I grab Lena's hand before she gets too far out of reach. "Wait."

Her eyes look down at our joined hands, a breath catching in her throat.

"Give me a kiss goodbye, and tell me you're mine."

Nervously, Lena looks around the patio, catching the occasional fucker looking our way.

"Julian." Her voice shakes. "Come on, you know I'm yours." Her eyes are still absently searching the patio. She cares. She cares what other people will think. She cares what they will think of her if they hear it.

But I don't. "Say it, Lena. Fucking say it." My voice is heavy and thick, ladened with my desire to hear the words flowing from her sweet mouth.

Inhaling a sharp breath, she leans down, slowly placing a kiss on my lips. She tastes like strawberries.

Pulling back slightly, she keeps her face within inches of mine. Her eyes dart between mine as she whispers, "I'm yours."

Even as she walks away, leaving me sitting on the patio of the café, I can hear the reluctance in her voice still ringing in my ears.

The thing is, I'm not angry. I could be angry for so many things. I could be angry with Lena for pretending this past week, for pretending our relationship was the same it has been these past two years. She played me well.

But seeing Logan's texts confirmed everything for me.

Yet there's one thing Lena seems to have forgotten. And that's how I won't tolerate being played, and I don't tolerate losing.

And considering all the variables, I know just what to do to remind her.

SEVEN

I take the opportunity to drop by Lena's apartment when she's at her hot yoga class. Between the class and the time it'll take for her to drive back home, I know I have roughly an hour. One hour to carry out my plan.

After I park my black BMW at the end of the parking lot, I jog my way up the stairs to Lena's apartment. The sun is still shining, and I'm thankful it isn't dark out. At this point, I don't give a shit who'll see me. I've been coming to Lena's apartment enough times in the past two years, I know no one will think twice about me being here.

Inserting my spare key, I turn the knob, unlocking the front door to her apartment.

Lena didn't exactly give me this key, per se. One night, about a year ago, I swiped her key when she was taking a nap at my apartment. I ran to the store and had a spare quickly made, knowing she was going to ask me if I wanted a copy, anyway.

Since then, I've had the key buried underneath a stack of paperwork in the center console of my car, keeping it for emergencies.

Emergencies such as this one.

When I step into the entryway of Lena's apartment, I inhale a deep breath. The mahogany teakwood scented candle sitting in the middle of the coffee table still lingers in the air. The wax hasn't even fully solidified yet, a thin layer of warm liquid still sitting on top. I drop my keys on the end table and swiftly make my way to Lena's bedroom.

My feet land on the plush grey rug lining the floor. Her room is quiet, eerily quiet. Everything in Lena's room is a bright white —from the dresser to the nightstand to the sheets covering her king size bed—the only exception the metal bed frame.

I smooth my hand along the metal arch of her bed frame. Sliding my hand into my pocket, I pull out the tie I used around Lena's wrists. Tying it to the headboard just like I did the other day, my cock hardens thinking about the way it felt to be inside her. The way it felt to have her legs spread, her arms tied above her, and my mouth covering every inch of her bare skin. With the tie still wrapped around the frame, I slide it between my fingers, release it, and let it hang there.

I unzip my pants and close my eyes, imagining the way Lena's body moved beneath mine, shivering with the pleasure I had given her. I wrap my hand around my erection, stroking myself. My knees press into Lena's mattress. With my free hand, I grip the bedframe, the cold metal pressing against my palm.

My legs tingle, the blood flowing through me. My heart races, remembering the way it felt to be inside Lena, to have her legs wrapped around my waist, my hips slamming into hers. My hand moves faster, and I release a heavy groan from my chest. The room is still utterly silent, the only sound the shallow quick breaths passing my lips in pleasure.

My hand slides faster against my skin, all of my nerves blasting off like a sudden burst of fireworks. My cock pulsates against my palm. I think about Lena this morning at the café. I think about the way her mouth pressed against mine, tasting like the strawberry crepes she ate. Then as I feel myself start to come, I hear her words rushing through my ears.

I'm yours.

As if she were in the room with me, I reach my peak, allowing myself to fully feel the pleasure my own hand is giving me. I look down, watching as my hand moves back and forth, finishing my orgasm. Propping my hand against the wall, I hang my head low, taking a moment to catch my breath, watching how powerful the thoughts of Lena can be.

When my heart rate slows to normal, and my cock relaxes, I zip up my pants. I take another deep breath and look down, realizing I came all over one of Lena's pillowcases. I don't really give a shit, but being the decent boyfriend I know I am, I'll wash it and replace it with a fresh case later. I leave the tie wrapped around the bed frame, letting my fingers smooth over the fabric once more. I leave it for Lena as a favor, to remind her of the day we used it to tie her to the bed.

Resting my hands on my hips, I circle Lena's room. My body is still thrumming from my recent orgasm, the numbing pleasure leaving my body, slowly. When I don't immediately see what I came looking for, I decide I need to search a bit deeper.

I start with Lena's closet. After thumbing through her hangers, I turn my attention to the built-in shelves. Deep in the back, folded between a stack of sweaters, I find what I came for.

I leave her closet and walk out to the middle of her room, Logan's Boston Bruins shirt gripped in my hand. Grabbing a pair of scissors from her desk, I sit on the end of her bed. I unfold Logan's t-shirt, staring at the giant worn out 'B.' I think about Lena, then I think about Logan. Then I imagine the scenario in which Logan gave Lena this shirt.

Did she ask for it? Or did he offer to give it to her? How long has he had this shirt? Is Logan from Boston? Is that how they know each other? Is that one of the things they have in common?

My stomach turns, and the pressure returns behind my eyes. I want to beat the shit out of Logan for stealing my girlfriend. I want to rewind to a time where I wasn't the pissed off, jealous boyfriend. I want to go back to a time where I didn't feel like my perfect life was slipping away. I want to go back to the time where I didn't feel like my mind was starting to slowly dissipate.

Holding out Logan's shirt, I begin cutting straight through the big, ugly fucking 'B.' Clenching the fabric, I open the scissors again, slicing the fabric over and over again. My mind fades away, and everything fades to black. Once I'm finished, I scatter the shredded pieces of Logan's shirt on the floor in front of Lena's bed.

I place the scissors back into the drawer of Lena's desk.

Burying my hands deep into the pockets of my pants, I leave Lena's apartment, satisfied. My heart thrashes against my ribs, thrilled.

It doesn't hit me until I get to my car and see Lena's car pulling into her parking spot.

I never replaced the pillowcase on Lena's bed.

Oops.

EIGHT

The day my father died was the best day of my life.

When I was younger, I spent most of my life in fear of what my father might do. And I spent most of my life being told to never apologize to anyone for anything. The only exception to this rule was my father. So, yes, to be honest, the day he died was a fucking Godsend. A Goddamn blessing in my eyes.

As I grew older, it became easier to avoid my father. When I turned twelve, I started being able to take care of myself and create any excuse not to be home. I could spend the night at a friend's house, no one gave a shit. Most of the time, I ventured to any art exhibit or museum within a twenty-five-mile radius, hitching a ride with anyone who would be willing to give me a ride. And to no surprise, my parents didn't give a shit then either.

If I happen to be home, I soon learned the only way I could tolerate to be around my father was to drink with him. He'd stumble through that metal screen door, just like he had the day I spilled the milk on the carpet. The same day he gave me my first taste of whiskey.

That became the norm. That easily had become my life.

I'd drink with my father, showing up to school the next day either hungover or still drunk. Days turned into weeks, then weeks into months, my life a constant blur. It didn't take long for me to become a professional at hiding it. I still managed to make straight As and work on my art. Art had become a passion of mine, more so on the historical side of it. I wanted to study and learn all I could about history, dating back to the beginning of time. I wanted to immerse myself in the bliss that was anything art related—all of it.

I did anything and everything I could to get out of Baton Rouge, anything to get away from my father. I set out to follow my dream, despite my father's lack of direction in his own life. He didn't give a shit about me or my mother. Then again, my mother didn't give a shit about anyone either, much less herself.

But the day my father died, tripping on the sidewalk and stumbling into one of Baton Rouge's busiest streets, was one of the best days of my life. My father's death was somewhat poetic in a way. He died the same way he lived his life. Stumbling and falling down drunk. Only when he died, he literally fell into oncoming traffic.

Some could call me insensitive. Some could call me a horrible, uncaring son. But those who would call me that, never had to live with a father like mine.

The reason the day of my father's death was the best day of my life was it was the day I knew my life became someone else's. I became a new man. One in which I owned a BMW, wore suits every day and earned a bachelor's degree in Art History.

With graduation already done and over, my degree framed and sitting in my apartment, I'm ready to move on. I'm ready to become the man I fought so hard to become. Much like the day my father died, today gives me that same feeling. I know I've become a different man, a different person.

I press down on the gas, taking my speed up to eighty-five. We're driving down Interstate 95, north to Boston. Lena's sitting beside me, dressed in a long black cocktail dress. Her blonde hair is tied low, braided into a bun, and her lips are painted a deep red, the perfect contrast to her pale brown eyes. I reach over, resting my hand on her thigh, ignoring the way her leg twitches, and her shoulders tense.

She hasn't smiled in the past hour we've been on the road, but I haven't complained. I'm too excited about tonight to even care.

After the day I cut up Logan's t-shirt, I wasn't even worried if Lena would say anything or know I was in her apartment. It's not that I don't care about her—I fucking love her—but I didn't care, I wanted her to know it was me. Which after finding the scraps of Logan's shirt on the floor and my come on her pillowcase, I'm sure she had her suspicions. If she did, she never let on.

I'm thankful because I don't think I could take another bit of her attitude or secrets. And it means my plan worked. She needed to be reminded of who she belongs to. If she has any kind of notion it was me who cut up the shirt, Lena knows I won't tolerate her bullshit anymore—or her secrets.

Since the day I snuck into Lena's apartment when she was at her hot yoga class, I've watched her. I followed her to those fucking classes, still not understanding how someone could take a class like that. Makes no fucking sense to me. I followed her when she ran her errands and when she spent time with Abby. And the times I was with her, I never complained because I knew, as far as I could see, my plan had worked.

Lena had received the message loud and clear. She was done with Logan. Not once since that day have I seen him or heard his piece of shit car rumbling down the street. With that knowledge, I was able to breathe a sigh of relief. Logan was gone.

She knows she's mine, and I'll never let her go. She knows I love her.

"I did a little research this week." I glance over at Lena and find her face turned away from me. She doesn't move or indicate she's even listening. Despite this, I still continue, rolling my eyes back to the road. "Anyway, I did my research and found out there's going to be a lot of big-name artists here tonight."

"Yep."

"What's your deal?" Fire burns in my chest, and I tighten the grip with the one free hand I still have on the wheel.

"Nothing." She takes a deep breath and taps her finger against her knee, then shifts in her seat.

My hand is still gripping her knee and as my speed grows closer to ninety, the more the fire grows underneath my chest. I press my fingertips into Lena's knee, urging her to listen to me.

"Listen, Lena," I say through clenched teeth. "You better not fuck this up for me tonight."

"Okay," she sighs. She widens her eyes for a second, staring out at the road in front of us. She's speaking to me as she were a child, annoyed with my constant nagging.

We're growing closer to the museum, and my nerves are on high alert.

"I mean it."

Lena's hand wraps around mine, pushing it off her knee.

"Fuck, Julian. You're hurting me."

Twisting my mouth, I flex my hand, attempting to calm myself. I place both hands on the wheel and take the exit we need to get where we're going.

"I'm just saying, Lena. Don't be spend the entire night being a fucking bitch."

NINE

The Institute of Contemporary Art is unlike any museum I've ever seen. It's a far cry from the shit museums in Baton Rouge. Even the ones in Providence don't hold a candle to this one.

My heart races as I take the steps up to the main part of the museum. It sits just at the edge of the water, several small boats lining the tiny piers, the moon glistening against the nearly still water.

I wrap my hand around Lena's, pulling her along with me. I can tell she's still angry with me for what happened in the car, but the closer I get to the museum and this exhibit, the less I care. I'm not going to lose her. I know, deep in my gut, Logan is gone and no longer an issue. My main focus is what's laid out before me, getting to know other people like me.

Once we make it inside, we head straight for the main exhibition. I can sense Lena's hesitation, but the second we enter the room, she straightens her back and plasters on her best fake smile.

I laugh to myself, seeing right through her façade. Grinning at her, I find a small bit of satisfaction. Even if her smile is fake, I find pride in the fact she's listening to me. We need to make a good impression, we can't fuck this up.

As expected, we make our usual rounds, gazing at the various pieces of art surrounding us. This exhibit is unlike every other one I've seen. It even extends as far as the courtyard and the piers sitting on the edge of the water.

"Julian," Lena tugs on my hand. "I'm going to go check out that room we passed by when we first walked in." She's carrying a champagne glass in her free hand, her fingers wrapped around the bottom of the flute.

I tighten my grip on her hand. "No, I thought we'd take a look outside at the courtyard. There are some interesting sculptures I thought we could see."

"Okay." Her voice is small, but she does as I ask.

It doesn't take long to get to the courtyard. When we step outside, the night air is cool, but a lingering amount of humidity saturates the air. Moisture forms along my forehead, and I lift my hand, making sure my hair is still presentable.

I lead Lena out a few feet from the bottom of the stairs onto the freshly cut grass. Twinkling lights are strewn above, warming the space above us.

I stop us in front of a red sculpture. The color pops as Lena and I stare at the way it glistens under the lights. Lena doesn't speak, and neither do I. It's a beautiful sculpture, unlike any I've ever seen.

My eyes dance across it, studying its curves and lines. Attached to the bottom of the piece, a small metal plaque is screwed into the base.

Stretching by Allison Newbury ©2009

"It's made from recycled water bottles."

Turning around at the sound of the voice, a woman stands behind us, a champagne glass similar to Lena's resting in her hand.

Her long blonde hair is curled and pulled to the side, resting over one of her shoulders. She seems a bit older than us, I'd say at least ten years. I don't even need to hear her name to know who she is. She's one of the artists I read up on. She's also the same artist whose name is engraved on the plaque under the red sculpture.

"Water bottles?" Lena asks in awe. "That's amazing."

Allison wraps both hands around her champagne glass and steps up to her sculpture. "It really wasn't too difficult. I like to design my pieces using unconventional material."

I grin. "I admire your boldness."

Allison waves me off. "Stop, you don't need to say anymore." She shrugs. "You know, I've been an artist all my life,"—she looks between me and Lena— "so it's all second nature to me. Despite this little fact about me, I never really feel like I'm good enough. Like I'm deserving. You know what I mean?"

"No," I mutter with a laugh.

I look over at Lena, realizing at the same time I said no, she said yes.

Giving her a questioning look, she ignores me, keeping her eyes locked on Allison.

Allison smiles, trading glances between us before she turns to me. She holds out her hand.

"Allison Newbury."

I return her gesture, releasing Lena's hand.

"Julian Price. This is my girlfriend, Lena." Instead of grabbing back onto Lena's hand, I slide mine into my pocket. "I've heard about you, Ms. Newbury. You are exceptionally talented."

"Please, call me Allison."

"You're based in Dallas, aren't you?" I take a sip of my whiskey, watching Lena from the corner of my eye. She remains beside me, quiet and listening.

"I am," Allison nods. "I'm actually in the process of purchasing my own gallery in Downtown Dallas at the moment." She turns, gesturing to the tall red sculpture. "The museum transported this piece up for the exhibit, so I took a little break to come for opening night."

"I suppose congratulations are in order then."

"Thank you." Her eyes sparkle against the golden lights, her red dress matching her sculpture. "What about you two? Are you artists as well or just simply my admirers?"

My heart flutters with her giggle. I can't explain it, and I can't put my finger on it, but I feel like Allison was just the person I needed to see here tonight. She's my ticket.

"Lena and I just graduated a couple weeks ago. We're both art history majors."

"How wonderful. I guess congratulations are in order for you as well," Allison grins, displaying her perfectly straight teeth. She holds up her champagne glass, extending her arm as if to toast. Following suit, Lena and I both raise ours, tapping them against Allison's.

"To us," Allison says. "And to kicking ass."

"To kicking ass," I repeat, muttering the words against the lip of my whiskey glass. The caramel liquid slides across my tongue, and I internally sigh, feeling the satisfying burn making its way down my throat. My stomach warms.

I swallow the rest of my whiskey, waving down the waiter for another round. I turn back to Allison, intrigued by what she could have to offer me. Whether it be a contact or any opportunities, shit I'd even settle for a small bit of advice on where to go from here.

"So, Allison, how do you feel about the Dallas Museum of Art?"

Lena reaches out, resting her fingertips against my arm. My eyes move from her fingers, finding her eyes.

"Will you both excuse me?" she says in a hushed tone. "I need to use the restroom. I'll be right back."

I smile at Lena, she smiles back, her eyes light with amusement, and that's when I know.

Clever, clever girl.

"Okay, baby," I say, ignoring the twist I feel piercing my chest. "We'll be here."

Lena nervously trades glances between me and Allison. "Of course."

Lena leaves us without another word. I watch as she makes her way up the concrete steps, heading back into the museum.

"Would you like to walk with me, Julian? Take a look at the other pieces?"

The waiter from earlier returns with a small silver tray. I pick up the glass of champagne, handing it to Allison. Then I pick up my glass of whiskey, immediately bringing it to my lips to take a sip.

"I'd love to."

By the time I've made a complete go around the courtyard with Allison, I've realized two things.

The first is I like Allison and not particularly in a sexual way. I mean, for a woman in her thirties and someone who is older than me, she is pretty attractive. Definitely fuckable. But aside from her blonde hair, which I have to admit I'm a sucker for, she's one of the most intelligent people I've ever met.

The second thing I notice is Lena hasn't come back from the restroom by the time we've made a full pass around the courtyard. The same feeling and instinct I have about Lena creep up on me. I know something isn't fucking right, but I remain calm, remembering who is still well within my company.

I clench my fist and throw back the rest of my whiskey just as I feel Lena sidle up beside me.

"I apologize for taking so long." She's wearing her fake grin. Allison doesn't know it, but I do. Of course, I do. I can see right through Lena's bullshit. She turns to me. "I was pulled aside by another artist, and we got to talking."

"Oh yeah?" Allison chimes in. "Which one? There are so many here tonight."

"Um…" Lena nervously swallows, her eyes darting between me and Allison. I shove my clenched fist into my pocket and wait to see how Lena chooses to answer Allison. "His name was Scott, I believe."

"Scott Young?" Allison asks, taking a guess.

"Yes." Lena's face immediately lights up as she snaps her fingers. "Scott Young, that was his name." Lena lifts her empty champagne glass. "I think these might be getting to me a bit."

She plays off her comment with a laugh, Allison not far behind.

Soon, I find myself amused as well. Amused at how well Lena likes to play her bullshit game. She thinks she's won. She thinks she's fooled me, but I know better.

"Well," Allison beams, glancing around the courtyard. "I should be getting back to my mingling and socializing. Part of being one of the participating artists."

"Thank you, Allison." I hold out my hand for Allison. ""Thank you, Allison. It was very, very nice to meet you."

"Oh, it was my pleasure. I had a great time talking with you." Allison turns to Lena and gently places her hand on Lena's arm. "You've got a great man here. Not only is he devilishly handsome, but he's kind and intelligent as well." Allison tips her head to the side in my direction. "Don't let this one go."

Instead of uttering a single word, Lena just gives Allison a tight-lipped smile. That's it. A fucking, closed mouth, bullshit smile. Wow, she couldn't even give Allison a reply. She couldn't even fucking pretend.

The whiskey engulfs my entire body into flames and fury. I can't stand Lena's bullshit anymore. I just need to let Allison say her goodbye before I say anything to her.

"Julian," Allison turns to me. I keep my rage with Lena at bay. See, that's the difference between me and Lena. At least I can hide my true emotions long enough to remain cordial. At least I'm professional. I raise my eyebrows in anticipation of what Allison might say.

"If you're ever in the Dallas area, come stop by my gallery downtown," Allison offers. "I know a few people who work for the Dallas Museum of Art I could introduce you to. They would be lucky to have someone as special as you working with them."

"Really?" I ask, stunned. Yes, it fucking worked. I knew

someone would see how fucking spectacular I am. I knew Allison was the person I was meant to meet tonight.

She gives me and Lena each a nod. "I look forward to hearing from you again. You two have a wonderful evening."

"You too."

Allison leaves us and walks away, stopping to talk to a group of guests surrounding the outside bar.

I don't even hesitate before I spin around, pinning Lena with a stare. "You couldn't even fucking say anything? A simple 'thank you' would have sufficed."

Lena narrows her eyes and tightens her jaw.

"I'm sorry to disappoint you, Mr. Price. It's kind of becoming more difficult to spout out endless lies." Pinning me with one last glare, Lena slams her champagne glass on a bar height table beside us. Gathering the bottom of her dress, she stomps away, storming up the concrete steps leading to the building.

Fire burns in my chest—either that or it's the whiskey. Whichever it is, it doesn't stop me from following Lena all the way through the museum and back out to the parking lot. I'm not sure where she thinks she's going because she came with me.

I catch up to her just as she steps off the sidewalk. Reaching out, I grab her arm at the elbow, pulling her to a stop.

"Don't you fucking walk away from me."

"Get the fuck off me, Julian!"

Lena's hand wraps around mine, using her fingers to pry mine off of her. She's unsuccessful of course, and I can sense her panic rising. Her breaths become quick and shallow, her voice wavering as she begs me to stop.

Pressing my fingers deeper into her arm, I pull her body against mine, my mouth close to her forehead. She refuses to meet my eyes, but still, she looks up, feeling my hot breath blow against her skin.

"Get back inside, Lena."

"No," she cries out.

I pull on Lena again, trying to get her to start walking back toward the museum. I can't have her fuck this up for me, for us, and I can't have her making a scene. She needs to calm down.

"Hey, asshole! Let her go."

Looking up from Lena's panicked face, I find Logan running toward us, worry written across his face.

"What the fuck are you doing here?" I ask him.

My jaw ticks and my teeth pulsate with the constant grinding. The pressure in my head is about to nearly explode.

"Get the fuck off her, man. Let her go." Logan steps up behind Lena and pries my hand off hers.

Shocked, I let my hand fall away, trying to comprehend why he's even here. Lena let him go. She would have let him go. She loves me, not him.

"Listen, you motherfucker," I say. "This is between me and my girlfriend."

Logan moves Lena behind him as if to protect her from me. I scoff, thinking how ridiculous it looks. There's no reason Lena needs to be afraid of me. I wouldn't hurt her.

"Okay, Julian." Logan holds his hand out to me, his voice calm and steady. "Lena and I are going to leave quietly. All you need to do is go back inside and enjoy the exhibit."

"What?"

Logan hesitates, still using his arm to keep Lena behind him.

"Lena doesn't want to be with you anymore. You're free, okay? You can do whatever you want. Just leave her be."

I laugh, tilting my head up to the night sky. I spot several stars, dotted throughout the dark blue-black painted sky. It almost looks like a Van Gogh painting. I'm still laughing when I return my gaze to Logan and Lena. Lena's eyes peek around Logan's shoulder, her hand wrapped around his arm.

I take a deep breath and run my hand across my mouth, swallowing the whiskey taste still present on my tongue.

"Logan, right?" I don't bother waiting for an answer before I continue. I hadn't noticed until now, but Logan has slowly begun to back away from me. I spot his piece of shit, red car in the corner of my eye. I clear my throat and point at him. "Logan, you don't fucking tell me what to do. Lena's mine. And don't act like you have any fucking right to come here and start making demands of me," I sneer, curling the corner of my mouth. "It's not very gentleman like."

Logan shakes his head. "Come on, Julian. Let this go, and we can all part ways in peace."

"Peace?" I ask my voice echoing through the parking lot. "You want peace? Maybe... just maybe, I would have considered peace if I didn't find out you were fucking my girlfriend."

"I'm not *fucking* your girlfriend, Julian. You're crazy."

I laugh again. Really, Logan's little act of playing the naïve one in this whole situation is already getting kind of old.

"Don't talk to me like I'm fucking stupid. I've known about you two for a long time. Why do you think I cut up that hideous Boston Bruins shirt? So, how about you do us all a favor and admit to what you fucking did."

"You're wrong, Julian," Logan says.

It doesn't surprise me when Logan and Lena's faces remain unchanged at the mention of the t-shirt. They knew it was me. I left that tie for Lena to see. A mixture of frustration and pride swells in me.

Pride knowing my plan worked, they knew it was me. Frustration with the fact it clearly didn't get the message across like I had expected. Maybe I wasn't clear enough.

I furrow my eyebrows at Logan, wondering how in the hell I'm wrong.

"Your relationship is done, Julian," he grits out. "Accept it and move on."

I clench my fists tighter, my nails cutting into my palms once again.

Logan's stupid, disgusting face grows closer to mine, closing the distance between us.

"I would leave now, Julian, while you can still keep your egotistical, chauvinistic ego hidden behind your lies. We won't mention what you've done if you let this go. Now."

"And what exactly have I done, Lena?" I turn my attention to her.

Tears spill down Lena's cheeks, her face filled with worry.

"You broke into my apartment, Julian. What you did..." Her voice drifts off as she shakes her head. She closes her eyes, taking a deep breath. "You left me no choice."

"Lena," I scoff. "It's not considered breaking in when you have a key." Reaching into my pocket, I pull out my keys. I find hers, along with my apartment and car keys, and hold it out just to show her. Since I had the key made, I've kept it in my car, but coupled with my constant surveillance on Lena these past few weeks, it's been easier to keep it with the rest of my keys.

"What?" she asks on a breath. Her wide eyes focus on the key dangling from my fingers. "You have a key to my place?"

"Of course, I do," I say. "You're my girlfriend."

"Julian, I think you and I both know we haven't been an actual couple in a long time."

"Really?" I ask, arching my eyebrows. "That's not what it sounds like when I'm fucking you in your bed."

"I think that's enough." Logan steps forward, injecting himself into the situation. His comments are unnecessary and unwarranted.

"Shut the fuck up," I yell at him.

"See?" Lena interjects. "I don't even know how to talk to you anymore because you do this kind of shit, Julian. You fly off the handle. I couldn't do this with you anymore. I didn't know what to do."

"Oh yeah," I mutter with a humorless laugh. "I know, Lena. I heard you tell Abby all about your plan to leave me tonight."

Again, I've surprised her. And the feeling is fucking glorious.

"What the fuck is wrong with you, man?" I turn my head to see Logan walking toward me, his smug face growing closer. "It's pretty simple to understand. Lena wanted to leave you a long time ago, but she was afraid of what you might do to her. Now, be the bigger person and walk away. Leave."

I release a hot breath through my nose. The scent and flavor of the whiskey still flooding my bloodstream ignites my senses. I can't listen to Logan anymore. His voice rings in my ears causing my head to spin. The next thing I know, I'm raising my fist and using all my strength to get Logan out of my face.

The sound of crunching followed by his body falling back onto the black asphalt fills my ears. Lena lets out an ear-piercing shriek, yelling Logan's name as I bend down, connecting my fist with his face again.

We're in the middle of the parking lot as I kneel down, strad-dling Logan. My arm pumps back and forth, delivering blow after blow. At first, Logan fights back. His frantic hands reach up, clawing at my perfectly pristine white collared shirt. His nails scratch against the fabric resting against my chest. My tie, similar to the one I used on Lena, is still wrapped around my neck, the tail of it brushing against Logan's desperate body.

Blood spurts from Logan's nose and my knuckles connect to it once again. It doesn't take long for his arms and legs to fall slack beside him.

His eyes immediately swell, blood seeping out from the corners of his eyelids.

My breaths are heavy and frantic, the weight on my back slowly pushing down, harder and harder. The feeling is almost euphoric. I imagine Logan on top of Lena, fucking her the way I fuck her.

Then I hear his voice, repeating in my ear, telling me to leave Lena.

My stomach curdles, and my throat burns. Lena's shaking hands wrap around my shoulders. My punches have slowed. I'm exhausted, and when I look down at Logan, his body beneath mine, there isn't a spot of skin that isn't splattered with blood. My knuckles are split from the force I used against every inch of his face.

"Julian, stop," Lena begs. "You're killing him."

Knowing Logan isn't able to run away from me now, and he can't take Lena away from me, I move to stand. I stumble, my foot catching on Logan as I stand. My body is shaking as I attempt to step toward Lena, the blood still rushing in my veins.

Lena immediately kneels beside Logan, resting her hand on his stomach. With her other hand, she smooths it along his cheek, painting her own hand with his blood. She's weeping, her shoulders shuddering with every sob.

"Logan... you're okay, baby. It'll be okay." She feels his chest, then looks up with frantic, panic-stricken eyes. She looks up at the small crowd, gathered near the front entrance.

"Somebody, call for help!" she yells.

I place both of my hands on my hips and step toward Lena.

"Lena," I clear the lump from my throat, my eyes averting the damage I've done to Logan. "Come on, let's go back inside. We're making a scene."

Panic twists in my chest, afraid of how many people saw what I did. I can't jeopardize my career. I can't let Logan be the reason my career goes to shit.

Lena stands up, her eyes filled with fire. She stomps her way to me. Her hand meets the side of my face, the crack of her skin slapping against mine ringing through my ears. My cheek burns, the ghost of her hand lingering on my skin.

She clenches her teeth, tears still spilling down her face.

"Get the fuck away from me!" she seethes.

"Lena," I sigh.

"No, Julian," she chokes out between sobs. She takes a deep breath, steadying herself. "You used to be a good person, but that was years ago. Somehow, I saw our relationship slowly dissipate. And you're nothing, nothing like the man I used to know. You're *nothing*."

Sirens wail in the background, red and blue flashing lights dancing across the concrete walls of the museum.

My eyes scan the crowd, then back to Lena. I'm not exactly

sure I'm comprehending what she's saying. I'm the same man I always was. How could she not see that? When did we get here?

"You better go, Julian." A tear spills from Lena's face as she slowly starts to back away, back to Logan. "Go now because as soon as the police get here, I won't hesitate to tell them you tried to kill Logan."

My eyes dart from Logan, still unmoving like a mannequin lying on the concrete to the ambulance speeding into the lot to Lena's grief-stricken eyes.

"Lena, I'm sor—" The words catch in my throat before I remember my father's number one rule.

"No," she says, cutting me off. "Don't. Just go. Leave, Julian and never look back. Start a new life. One far from here and one that doesn't involve me."

Then as the paramedics jump from the ambulance, surrounding Logan's near lifeless body, I turn and run. I run away from the man I used to be, to the new man I'd become.

WANT THE NEXT BOOK?

Continue reading for an excerpt from Brittany Taylor's, *Mine,* the
next book in the Back to Me Series!

LENA

The crunching beneath my foot feels like a million bones snapping all at once.

"Well, shit." I groan, bending down to pick up the remnants of what was once my phone. The shattered screen and half-broken backing bend across the palm of my hand like a sad, spineless mess. Wiping large clumps of mud and rain from the screen, I foolishly try to turn it back on knowing there's no possible way it could still work.

When it doesn't come back to life, I snap my head up at the sound of a car door closing. Logan's footsteps pound into the soaking wet asphalt as he steps up onto the curb, stopping in front of me.

Concerned, he eyes the shattered remains of my phone. "Again, Lena?", he sighs, cradling my hands in his. Heavy drops of water cover the skin of our joined hands. I look up at him between rain-soaked eye lashes.

"I know." A piece of me deflates, knowing I've only had this phone for two months. However, the last phone was replaced simply out of necessity and survival than it was pure clumsiness. "I can't help it," I say. "I tripped getting out of the car." I glance over my shoulder, narrowing my eyes at the exact spot I tripped.

Logan swipes his thumb along my cheek, pulling my gaze back to him. "Always so clumsy."

I laugh. "No. I think it's just a case of bad luck."

We're standing on the sidewalk outside Logan's apartment in the center of Providence. Thick, heavy drops of rain continue to pour down on us, soaking us from head to toe. The sound of passing cars, their tires barreling through puddles, echoes behind us. Logan's touch stirs me, bringing back those all too familiar warm feelings in the bottom of my stomach. His thumb grazing my skin matches the warm water saturating our skin.

I'm still holding my broken phone in my hand when I raise my other one to his head. I brush my fingers against the freshly cut strands. His chestnut colored hair now looks black thanks to the thunderstorm brewing above us. The ends are pressed against his forehead, weighed down by the cool water. His hair is cut short and a piece of me deflates, missing the way it used to look, long and unruly. But just like my first replacement phone, Logan cut his hair out of necessity.

I run my hand down the side of his face then slide it across his waist, wrapping my arm around his sculpted frame. His muscles instinctively retract at my touch and I can't deny how my stomach flutters knowing I still elicit this kind of reaction out of him. It's only been a few months since Logan and I have really been together and not a day has passed where I don't remember how much I love him. I scan his face, my heart fluttering as his mouth turns up into a smile. His jaw is covered in the beginnings of a beard, the scruff hiding the leftover evidence of what his face had endured several months ago. Scars are buried underneath, a constant reminder of how I had nearly lost him.

Logan wraps his hands around my waist, gripping onto my hips. He pulls me close and the familiar scent of orange tic-tacs fills the moisture filled air between us. Ever since I met him, he's been absolutely obsessed with orange tic-tacs. Claims they're the only one's worth eating. I always thought it more had to do with the fact that he quit smoking just after I met him, and he knew it was the only thing that kept him from picking up the habit again. That and the fact that they were significantly cheaper.

His eyes search my face. "We should probably get inside. We're getting soaked."

"I don't care." I laugh. Thunder rumbles the sky above us and my heart skips a beat, the feeling shooting straight through me.

"Come on." Logan laughs, tucking a few loose strands of hair back behind my ears. His fingers stop short when he reaches the ends. As Logan had done, I cut my hair as well. Not too short, but enough for me to be able to feel the absence of the weight it once held. He grabs the shattered remains of my phone and drops them into the grocery bag he's holding. He wraps his arm around me, urging me to follow him inside to his apartment. "We'll get you a new phone tomorrow."

Logan's apartment building is tall. It's one of those apartment buildings that require a security code to get in the front door. One large door remains as the only entrance into the building, its brick exterior acting as a blanket of security. When Logan had recovered enough to be released from the hospital, both of us had decided it would be best for us to stay together, to live together. His recovery was going to be a long process, one that would take up the majority of my time. Neither of us felt safe anymore and as far as we knew, Julian didn't know where Logan lived. In the time that Logan was recovering in the hospital, I would stay with him as much as I possibly could, or I would stay with my best friend, Abby. I didn't feel safe returning my apartment, knowing my ex-boyfriend knew where I lived.

"So, what will it be tonight?" Logan enters the code into the small silver box beside the front door to the building. I follow him as he steps inside. He begins walking backward toward the elevator, lifting the now soggy brown paper bag of groceries. His mouth curls back into that playful smirk. His golden eyes spark and I can feel them consuming me. "Spaghetti or tacos?"

I twist my face in disgust. Laughing, I step into the elevator, pressing the button for the nineteenth floor. "Spaghetti? Are you really asking me to choose between spaghetti and tacos? Hands down you know I'm choosing tacos." I reach up, squeezing the excess rainwater from my hair then lean against the wall, eyeing Logan from across the small space between us.

"I knew it wasn't a contest. I'm just a sucker for when you twist your face the way you just did. The way your smooth lips twist at the perfect angle. The way your eyebrows slant into those gorgeous green eyes of yours." His eyes gleam despite the dim lights overhead as he slowly says each word. He leans back against the opposite wall, tipping his head back, mimicking my stance and watching me with hooded eyes. He's happy. I'm happy.

Pushing off the elevator wall, I walk across the small space, tipping my chin up to meet Logan's gaze. I press my hips into his, melting into his body. I grasp onto the wet fabric of his shirt with my fingers and run my tongue across my lip, pulling him impossibly closer. "And I'm a sucker for you, Logan Moore."

Logan reaches up, wrapping his hand on the back of my head. His movements are quick, as if he knows exactly what he's doing. His fingers thread through my wet hair. He pulls me close, pressing my lips to his. His mouth is warm and wet from the rain. I sigh against his body. His hand slides away from my hair and along my cheek, holding me back just enough for me to see his face. "I want it to be like this forever, Lena."

"Me too."

Then, as the elevator dings, reaching the nineteenth floor, I will Logan's words to be true. I wish I could freeze this moment in time. One where my heart feels like it might burst out of my chest and Logan's staring at me like he wouldn't want to ever be looking at another person for the rest of his life.

I playfully bump my shoulder into his solid, sculpted arm as we step out into the hallway. It's quiet as it usually is, and I'm thrilled about the prospect of removing my rain-soaked clothes. My cheeks grow sore from grinning as Logan walks ahead of me. My smile immediately fades when I stumble and nearly trip into his, the right side of my body slamming into his. His body is stiff, frozen solid and every part of my body turns cold when I follow his gaze.

The door to Logan's apartment is propped open, six inches of black empty space between it and the doorframe. We both don't immediately walk toward the door. Instead, he reaches his arm out, blocking me from walking further than where he is standing. He's protecting me, unsure what kind of situation we're in.

"Wait here." Logan whispers.

"No." I whisper back. "I'm going with you." I wrap my hands around his arm, pressing my fingers into his tensed muscle.

He narrows his gaze toward me for a moment, knowing how stubborn I can be.

A chill prickles down the back of my neck and a familiar feeling washes over me. Fear pierces its way into my chest. Logan's heavy boots carefully step onto the carpet as we inch forward, carefully examining what type of situation we're walking into.

We've been here before. Months ago, I walked into my apartment to find Logan's Boston Bruins t-shirt shredded to pieces on my bedroom floor and my ex-boyfriend's tie knotted to the metal post of my bed frame.

I close my eyes and take a deep breath, willing myself to believe this isn't the same. This can't be Julian. It can't.

When we make it to the front door, leans forward and carefully peeks through the opening, before gently nudging the door open with the tip of his boot. The hallway leading to the living room is pitch black and after my eyes have taken a moment to adjust, it doesn't appear as if anything has been disturbed. But the sight doesn't bring any sense of relief. It's Julian's way. He has a way of letting you know he's there without making it obvious.

Neither of us step into the apartment and I could swear I could hear Logan's heart pounding alongside mine, echoing through the empty hallway. I suddenly remember just how alone we are. I hold my breath, the oxygen swelling in my neck as I turn my head, glancing down each side of the hallway. There's no one that I can see. Again, there's no relief, worried the person could still be inside.

"I'm going to check inside the apartment and make sure there isn't anyone still in there. I need you to stay here."

"No." I shake my head. "I'm going in there with you." I remove his hands from my face, holding them between us. "I'm safer with you than I am standing out here alone."

He presses his lips into a thin line, nodding in acknowledgement. I can see the war in Logan's eyes. He's afraid. He's not afraid of what is inside the apartment. Instead, he's more afraid of how what's inside will affect me. He's worried for me.

I look into Logan's eyes one more time, silently telling him I'm ready to go inside. Without another word, he turns around and takes one careful step inside, craning his head farther into the apartment hoping to get a better view.

I'm immediately darting my eyes across every surface, looking for any clue that Julian may have been in our apartment.

I grip onto Logan's hand tighter as we walk deeper into our apartment. Not one single item in the living room or kitchen looks disturbed, still in the same place it was when Logan and I had left hours before. Logan stops in the living room, placing the wet grocery bag on the coffee table. He turns to face me, still holding onto my hand. "No one's in here." His whispered voice is a contradiction to his words. Even he doesn't believe we're safe. He knows something, or someone, is here. The apartment feels as if all the life has been sucked out of it. The darkness pouring into every corner of every room.

A brief wave of foolish relief hits me before I remember that we still need to check the rest of the apartment, including our bedroom and the bathroom. Logan leads us down the hallway and almost immediately I spot something sitting on top of the tightly made bed. My stomach twists and the chills return to the back of my neck, only this time it feels like tiny pin pricks dancing all the way down my spine. I already know what it is before I've fully seen it.

In the center of the bed is a neatly folded t-shirt. The fabric is pressed and folded into a perfect square, not a single wrinkle. In the center of the black t-shirt is a large letter 'B'. The Boston Bruins logo. On the top of the shirt is a folded note.

"No." I cover my mouth with my hand then turn to Logan with wide panic-stricken eyes.

His eyes are just as wide as mine only they're steeled on the shirt and note resting on our bed. He doesn't speak a word. I stand in silence, watching as his jaw ticks. I can see the thoughts running through his mind. He's deciding what to do.

I reach for the taped note with a trembling hand. My rain soaked, nervous fingers reach out, pinching the thin sheet between them.

I jump when I feel a tap on my arm. I gasp for air when I turn around, realizing it was Logan. He raises his finger to his mouth, reminding me to stay quiet. Staying silent, he gently nods his head toward my hand, his eyebrows bending in confusion. I'm still holding the note between both two fingers. I'm holding it as if it contains some sort of poison or deadly virus. Its weight grows with every passing second, the heaviness quickly becoming too much for me to handle. Panic rises inside me and the feeling is all too familiar. My stomach twists with every painful heartbeat pounding in my chest.

Logan's eyes move to the note in my hand. Our clothes are still soaked from the rain yet the short strands of Logan's hair have already completely dried. Rain droplets are still dotted across his skin, dripping their way down with every nervous breath he takes.

The thin paper is an off-white color and I quickly recognize it. It's a piece of paper from one of my sketch books. Aside from the words written inside, it's completely blank, unused.

I hold my breath as I slowly open the folded paper and gasp when I read the words written in bold ink.

You should have known I wouldn't give up so easily. You may have moved on, but one thing hasn't changed. You're still MINE.

"What does it say?" Logan's eyes are steeled on me, his face tense as he waits for me to respond. When I don't, he asks again. "Lena. What does it say?"

"I can't..." My breaths begin to quicken and my throat swells. It's becoming harder to breath and the longer I keep my feet planted where they are the more I'm allowing the panic to overtake me. I lift my arms and run my fingers through my hair, hoping it will somehow relieve the pressure on my chest and the sickness brewing inside me. "I..."

Logan rips the note from my shaking hands when I don't answer him and immediately begins reading the note. Wide eyed, he snaps his head up, the message clearly injecting fear into him the same way it had for me. "We have to leave."

"Leave?" I'm hearing Logan but his words fall on deaf ears. I don't understand him.

"Yes. We need to get out of here. We aren't safe here anymore." Logan sets the wet grocery bag on the floor beside his feet then turns to me. He grips my face in his hands, his fingers catching the silent tears streaming down my face. I hadn't realized that I was already crying.

"Look at me, Lena." Logan's attempting to calm my nerves and when my eyes meet his I'm stunned to see his so determined. He's definitely more rational and aware than I am right now.

"We have to go." Then as if he flipped a switch, he moves quickly, taking large steps to the closet. Within seconds he tosses my pink overnight bag to me then begins filling his black backpack.

I'm holding the note still staring at the shirt as if I'm expecting it to suddenly spring to life and jump off the bed.

"Lena." Logan's hand is suddenly on my shoulder. It sounds like his voice is under water. "I know it's hard but we have to go."

"He was supposed to be gone. I gave him the chance to start over." I face Logan with tear filled eyes and swallow the lump in my throat. "Where are we going to go, Logan?" Worry begins to replace the panic and time starts to slow down.

"Look, Lena. I know this is really difficult right now but we need to go." Logan points to the shirt. "This is clearly Julian sending a message. He knows where we live and we're no longer safe here. We need to go and we need to do it fast."

I look away from Logan and back down to the shirt. The logo is slightly different than the one Julian had cut into pieces and left at the foot of my bed. Logan had given me the shirt when I had told him I wanted to leave Julian and be with him. My only problem was that I didn't know how to safely leave him. Apparently, it didn't matter how I'd left him. He would always be in my life whether I wanted him or not.

My chest aches but I take a deep breath, unwilling to find out what Julian might do if we don't.

I cross the room to Logan's closet and start pulling every shirt and dress I can see, shoving it deep into my bag. I'm about to head into the bathroom when I realize the last piece of clothing I'd grabbed was a dark maroon sweater. The subtle scent of menthol wafts from the top of my bag as I lift the sweater, staring at it in my hand. I slide my fingers across the maroon fabric and remember how I ended up with this sweater. Abby's favorite cardigan.

It was mid-January and we were standing outside our favorite café in Providence. It wasn't snowing but I remember the way the cold air seeped its way into my bones. Abby inhaled one last deep drag of her cigarette then turned to me as I wrapped my arms around myself, attempting to rub the chill off them.

"I thought the cold didn't bother you, Boston girl."

She was teasing me as she always did. Abby was originally from the west coast so she always picked on me for being a stuck-up New Englander. I always teased her for being a clueless valley girl from southern California. I was surprised the cold hadn't bothered her but that could be due to the fact she was always prepared, covered head to toe in winter gear.

"It doesn't bother me." I told her, rolling my eyes. "I just forgot how cold it was supposed to be today. I didn't check the weather."

Abby sighed, smashing her toe on the concrete, crushing what was left of her cigarette. "Here, take my sweater." She quickly shrugged her sweater off.

"Seriously, Abby. I'm fine." I held my hand out, telling her not to worry.

"Take it." She urged, widening her violet eyes. "I want you to have it."

I paused, considering whether I should take it or not. It was her favorite sweater but the frigid air biting my skin won out. "Fine." I groaned, thankful to have a best friend who was as persistent as she was. Even if it was only a simple sweater.

Now, as I smell the last remnants of Abby's cigarette embedded in the sweater, I realize I probably won't ever see her again, knowing it's the only way to make sure she's safe.

Anger starts to overtake the worry. Julian has managed to destroy every piece of my life. He not only nearly ended Logan's life; he's also causing me to leave behind the only other person I still care about. Abby.

"Len." Logan's hand grips my arm, pulling me toward the front door of the apartment. I look down and see he's already gathered my things from the bathroom. "We have to go. Now."

I follow Logan out of the apartment not knowing where we're headed or how far we'll need to go to feel safe. By the time we've reached the elevator I begin to realize I may never feel safe again.

Want to read more of *Mine*? Continue the series and grab your copy on Amazon:

Mine: A Back to Series Book 2: https://amzn.to/31bvzfV

FOLLOW BRITTANY

Want to stay in the loop?
   Join my reader group-
   https://bit.ly/36QAWSZ

Visit my website and sign up for my newsletter:
   Website: www.brittanytaylorbooks.com

ACKNOWLEDGMENTS

As with every book, I would like to thank my family and my friends. You guys remind me every day of why I love doing what I do. Your encouragement and support mean the world. I owe an enormous thank you to my best friend and fellow author, Ashley Munoz. Seriously, Ashley, I can never thank you enough for your support and friendship. The amazing thing is that we've continued our friendship between a three thousand mile distance. But distance doesn't matter. And that's what makes our friendship so special. Thank you for pushing me with this novella. For giving me the gentle nudge I needed to push my boundaries and to take the risks, reminding me that I'm writing Julian's story. And that Julian doesn't give a fuck. (Insert evil laugh here) This book would not be what it is without you. Thank you to all my readers and the readers in my group, Book Beauties. You guys absolutely rock. It's amazing how this tiny book, my shortest to date, has changed me as a writer. Julian challenged me and made me question my thought process sometimes. Some of his experiences downright made me cringe. But as much as everyone hates him, and rightfully so, I fucking love him.

Printed in Great Britain
by Amazon

59734026R00064